TWO BROTHERS

A Novel by Mark C. Iampietro

Copyright © 2025 by Mark C. Iampietro

All rights reserved.

No part of this publication may be reproduced, distributed, or transmitted in any form or by any means, including photocopying, recording, or other electronic or mechanical methods, or conveyed via the internet or a website without the prior written permission of the author. All rights inquiries should be directed to marco1114@rcn.com

Disclaimer

This is a work of fiction. Unless otherwise indicated, all the names, characters, businesses, places, events and incidents in this book are either the product of the author's imagination or used in a fictitious manner. Any resemblance to actual persons, living or dead, or actual events is purely coincidental.

Synopsis

"Two Brothers" explores the differences which may occur between siblings. Stark differences caused by genetics or environment sometimes play a role, but it also explores the matters of Fate and Destiny. Fate is described as a predetermined course of events that are inevitable and usually adverse, and Destiny implies choices that result in positivity.

The mid-1890s saw Salvatore Arcuri fleeing Sicily after an impulsive decision led to the destruction of their family's organization and the deaths of those they held dear. Escaping death, he hid in a tiny hamlet in Campania, where he met and married a young woman named Concetta. But Salvatore knew that the small, isolated town could not contain his criminal ambitions. He was heir to his father's criminal throne, and he would make his way to America, through Ellis Island. Following another's advice, he relocated to South Bethlehem, Pennsylvania, where, sensing opportunities, he established a new version of his father's criminal enterprises. He would master the vices of men, cynically taking advantage of human frailties, and purchase political and legal protection through corruption.

Meanwhile, also forced to flee, younger brother Nico's early years in America were hard. He found work as a custodian, sweeping floors, while Salvatore thrived in his growing criminal empire. Every night, Nico studied, and took advantage of opportunities in his adopted home to become a lawyer.

Salvatore's world remained one of shadows, an unbreakable tie to their past that neither could fully sever. He used corruption to influence events to his criminal favor.

Nico Arcuri's legacy was built not just on his success but on his integrity. He never bent to corruption, never forgot the struggles of his youth, and never stopped fighting for those without a voice. His name became synonymous with justice.

"Two Brothers" ultimately tells how one brother's decisions shaped the other's destiny.

Prologue

Victoria Maria Teggiano O'Brien's long search for her family's origins led her to Bethlehem, Pennsylvania, thanks to a popular genealogy website. She became connected with the pastor of the Holy Infancy parish, which had an unofficial link to the oldest Catholic cemetery in the city. For Victoria, this cemetery might offer her the last chance to trace the mysterious great-grandfather about whom so much had been hidden. When she inquired about the cemetery's burial records, the pastor was brutally honest, telling her that, to his knowledge, none existed. Sensing her disappointment, he offered a glimmer of hope: "Emilio Diana might have some knowledge," he said. According to the pastor, Emilio had an almost encyclopedic knowledge of South Bethlehem and its Italian community specifically.

Victoria's genealogical search began quite accidentally a few years earlier. The unexpected death of her husband and her retirement the previous year provided her with some of the motivation she needed to embark on this journey. Naturally a busy person, Victoria realized she needed something to keep her mind engaged. As a childless widow at the age of sixty-five, she spent the first several months grieving her husband's sudden passing. Although she engaged in volunteer work and caught up on her reading, these activities were not enough to fully occupy her time.

One day, she stumbled upon a website dedicated to genealogy. Curious, she explored the site and found many of the stories compelling. People like her were connecting with their past through research, and the Internet made this process much easier. Eventually, she felt bold enough to join the site and interact with others. Following the advice of a friend, Victoria entered as many names as she could think of to cast a wide net. Along with her maiden name, she decided to include the name "Arcuri," which had come up several times in her past. To her surprise, she soon received a message from a young woman in Italy. The woman's last name was Morano, and she lived in Ragusa, Sicily. Through this contact, Victoria learned about a family named Arcuri with ties to Ragusa. Their conversation piqued Victoria's curiosity about whether her great-grandfather originated from that town. The contact knew a town official who could help, and for a small fee, the official—who had access to birth, death, and marriage records—was able to connect Victoria to her pre-American roots.

Thanks to an official document, Victoria's family lineage could now be traced across two continents and over a century. From a young age, Victoria sensed that various aspects of her family history were intentionally kept hidden. She was born Victoria Maria Teggiano in Enfield, Connecticut, in 1949. Apart from her name, there was little else she knew about her family's origins. Like many Americans of her generation—known as Baby Boomers—she was quite removed from her great-grandparents roots. Victoria knew that her parents were born in America, but she had little information about her great-grandparents, particularly on her father's side. She inferred that her family had emigrated from "somewhere in Italy," but the vague answers she received whenever she asked left her with more questions than answers. Her research uncovered some information but also revealed mysterious gaps. These gaps eventually led her to Bethlehem.

The elderly man who answered the knock at the door was named Emilio Diana. He was a parochial vicar and deacon at the now-defunct Italian church in South Bethlehem. Emilio was a kind man, likely over ninety years old, and by this time, he was in failing health. Victoria felt fortunate to have found someone from his generation to assist her. After exchanging greetings, Emilio proudly described himself as an immigrant, having arrived "many years ago." With his distinct accent, he explained that due to his connection to the church, he had become familiar with Saint Michael's Cemetery. He even boasted that as a young man, he could easily navigate the rough terrain and claimed to know "every inch" of the burial grounds, confirming what the priest had mentioned. Emilio lived in a modest home on Atlantic Street, a narrow row house typical of those built more than a hundred years ago to house industrial workers who had flocked to South Bethlehem from all over Europe.

"You see, I have been able to trace my lineage as a 'Treggiano,'" Victoria began. "However, I cannot seem to find many details concerning my great-grandfather, who may have been named Arcuri." At this point, the old man went to a drawer and retrieved a blank piece of writing paper. With a well-worn pencil, he invited the younger woman to join him at his small kitchen table and began sketching out a map, hoping it would lead Victoria to her family's past. He completed the map in about five minutes and then took time to describe the best approach. "From State Street, past the Castellucci mausoleum, head up the brick path for about one hundred yards," he explained. "There you will no longer be on a path but continue straight on the bare ground. Be careful, as it is very hilly and can be dangerous," he cautioned. Victoria accepted the man's generosity and thanked him. She folded the map and placed it into her coat pocket. Emilio wished her well and said, "I hope you find what you are seeking and that you do not experience disappointment."

Victoria easily located Saint Michael's, as it was no more than a mile from Emilio's house. She parked her car as close to the State Street entrance as possible to avoid the treacherous, slippery surfaces that surrounded her on that day. Although she was in fine condition for a sixty-six-year-old, Victoria was acutely aware of the dangers of falling. The late winter wind swept across the stark expanse of the old cemetery, prompting Victoria to cinch her coat tightly around her neck. With the wind factored in, the temperature on this early March morning was in the teens. Remnants of the long, cold season lingered along the path through the ancient burial ground, with snow still present in nearly every shaded section of Saint Michael's cemetery. As she entered the graveyard, the old man's final words haunted Victoria: "I hope you don't find disappointment." Did she misinterpret what he meant? Perhaps his broken English contributed to her confusion. She walked slowly uphill, mindful of the slick and uneven cobblestone surface. To her left, the steep slope of the land descended toward Fourth Street, while to her right, a long, steep climb led to the upper reaches of the property and the edge of a forest.

What awaited her? Answers or more questions? After ten minutes of searching, struggling against the slippery ground and bitter winds, Victoria considered giving up. But something deep inside urged her on. "You've come too far," she said to herself. Eventually, her determination paid off. She spotted a modest, well-worn stone inscribed, "Qui giace Salvatore Arcuri 1870-1929." "Short and sweet," she thought. Using her phone, she took pictures from various angles before heading back down the hillside to her car. Suddenly, she paused, turned back, and said an Our Father. As she warmed up in her car, sipping black coffee from her

Thermos, Victoria reviewed the progress she had made on her family project.

Victoria felt disconnected from her Italian heritage as her family seemed to shy away from their roots. Her parents, lapsed Catholics, rarely mentioned their great-grandparents, and Italy was rarely acknowledged in their home life. Intrigued by her great-grandfather's origins, Victoria sensed a mix of curiosity and dread as she delved into her family's history. She easily traced her lineage through her parents to her paternal grandparents, both born in America. However, her research hit several unexplained bumps around the turn of the century.

Why did the family surname change from "Arcuri" to "Teggiano," and what made this a family taboo? Her maiden name was Teggiano, but she found no records of anyone named Arcuri before around 1925, when her father was born. Quite by accident, she discovered that a name change likely occurred during her great-grandfather's time. If that is the case, what prompted it? Was there something to be ashamed of?

Table of Contents

Synopsis iv

Prologue vi

Chapter 1: Sicily 1

Chapter 2: A Pivotal Decision 7

Chapter 3: Repercussions 11

Chapter 4: Vendetta 22

Chapter 5: Fateful Decision 27

Chapter 6: Harsh Reality 31

Chapter 7: Journey to Campania 36

Chapter 8: Introduction to Foiano di Val Fortore 42

Chapter 9: Changes 48

Chapter 10: A Turn of Events 58

Chapter 11: Eighteen Ninety-Four 69

Chapter 12: Concetta Maria 75

Chapter 13: Blowback 85

Chapter 14: Marriage 88

Chapter 15: Cape Passero 92

Chapter 16: Gio Establishes Himself 96

Chapter 17: Finalizing a Plan 100

Chapter 18: Uncertainty 106

Chapter 19: Lombardia 111

Chapter 20: Two Journeys to America 115

Chapter 21: Establishment in South Bethlehem 122

Chapter 22: Nico Blossoms 133

Chapter 23: Eighteen Ninety-Seven 143

Chapter 24: Two Brothers, Two Very Different Paths 150

Chapter 25: Nineteen-Twenty-Nine 167

Author's Note 174

About the Author 176

Chapter 1:

Sicily

Salvatore Arcuri was born into poverty. His family's background was steeped in hardship, a common experience in old Italy. During the 19th century, as the country struggled to transition from feudalism, many unfortunate families were left behind. The Arcuri family belonged to the peasantry classified as "have nots." In Sicily, between 1800 and 1870, land barons and the church controlled valuable land. Southern Italy, including Sicily and Sardinia, was primarily agricultural. While the barons deployed private armies to enforce the law, the new authorities failed to manage rising crime and expanding commerce. In the absence of effective law enforcement, people turned to extra-legal protectors, leading to the rise of the Mafia. In small towns and villages, especially in regions like Ragusa, where formal police forces were lacking, local leaders addressed banditry by recruiting young men into "companies at arms." These groups were tasked with hunting down thieves and negotiating the return of stolen property, saving communities the cost of training their own police. Salvatore Arcuri's father was one of these leaders. Francesco Salvatore Arcuri earned a reputation as a "man of honor" during this lawless period. He became known for achieving results for those who hired him, whether it involved retrieving stolen cattle or a harvest of lemons. Nicknamed "Il Leone," he gained respect as a leader in the Ragusa area, which stretched from west of Siracusa to Vizzini in the north, westward toward Comiso, and at its height, south to Pozzallo. Born into poverty around 1840 in the village of Castellucia in the Ragusa region of southeastern Sicily, Francesco was determined not to live hand-to-mouth. Instead, he resolved to take what he needed and never to rely on a corrupt system.

When Francesco became a father for the first time around 1870, he realized that by the time his son came of age, the boy would have to face a crucial decision about his future. Would he live as a pauper, or would he follow in his father's footsteps and become another "Il Leone"? From an early age, Francesco's first son, Salvatore Arcuri, demonstrated strong leadership qualities. By the time he turned twenty, Salvatore would face significant challenges that would test him. He was unusually tall for a Southern Italian, standing just over six feet. With slicked-back jet-black hair, sharp features, a hawk-like nose, piercing dark brown eyes, and a very dark beard, Salvatore always appeared as though he needed a shave. His broad shoulders and upright posture, with his chest thrust out, projected an image of a man in control. Salvatore began assisting in the family business as soon as his father deemed him worthy of responsibility. His specialty was extracting information from stubborn thieves, compelling them to reveal the locations of their accomplices and hidden stolen goods. Francesco recognized that his son was destined to continue the family tradition. In contrast, Francesco had no such expectations for his second son, Nico, who was seven years younger than Salvatore.

The two brothers were almost as different as night and day. Nico was slight in stature and had been sickly as a child, earning him the derision of his father, who referred to him as "il figlio di mamma," or "momma's boy." Consequently, Nico was seldom included in the manly pursuits that Francesco and Salvatore enjoyed, such as hunting, knife throwing, and firearms practice. From the outset, Nico felt the sting of rejection from both his father and his older brother. In 1893, the relatively peaceful existence of the Arcuri family was shattered by the assassination of Il Leone. For more than fifteen years, Francesco Arcuri had maintained a fragile peace in the southern Sicilian region under his influence. He earned a reputation as a man who could stand up to authorities and advocate for the peasants of Ragusa and the surrounding towns. His influence reached every town and village in the area. People from as far away as Scoglitta and Pedlino sought his wise counsel or, in some cases, his intervention when demanding justice. Revered by his local community and respected, if not feared, by others, he became known as Don Francesco.

Beginning early in his career, Don Francesco earned the respect of the farmers who owned the rich agricultural lands around Ragusa. He satisfied his clients' needs by tracking down the plundering thieves, and in return, the land barons gladly offered him rewards. Instead of accepting cash, he chose to receive gratuities such as "a piece of the business," or *pezzo dell'azienda*. This approach proved to be far more lucrative because it was open-ended; Don Francesco became a partner with the landowners rather than just a one-time beneficiary. If a landowner was reluctant to accept this form of payment, they might face unfortunate consequences—such as a mysterious barn fire, the disappearance of their wagons, or damage to their crops. Before long, Don Francesco recognized that he might as well change his business model to "Protezione," or protection. Consequently, the region's landowners were willing to provide gifts ranging from cash to pieces of land to avoid certain "misfortunes." Eventually, Don Francesco decided to expand his influence east toward the critical port city of Siracusa. Although he was already successful as the man who controlled the rich farmlands of southern Sicily, he yearned for more power. To understand his influence, one must grasp how he achieved it. Within the region of Ragusa, Don Francesco was the king of all he surveyed. His "family" consisted of his loyal son Salvatore and a few dozen men on his payroll. Some of these men were mercenaries, loyal only to whoever would pay them. Salvatore had graduated to the role of collector, traveling by horseback throughout Ragusa to gather tributes from the landowners. There was rarely any trouble—rarely. One evening, after supper in their home in Monterosso, Francesco revealed his plan to his son. "You know that greater riches await us on the coast?" To

Salvatore, this continuation of an idea that his father had been harboring for several years came as no surprise. Though happy and satisfied himself, Salvatore knew he did not possess the same level of drive as his father. It seemed that Francesco could never be satisfied by wealth and power alone. What else was he after? "Father, I respect and love you, but I do not understand your need to go to Siracusa..." "My son," Francesco replied, "I love and respect you as well, but any truly great man is never satisfied with his successes." He paused and took a long drag on his cigar.

The Don laid a map of Sicily on the wooden table, clearing away plates of food. "Here..." he pointed to the southeast. "Siracusa!" he exclaimed, animated. "Its importance is hard to explain." "We have Ragusa," he continued, circling it. "But with Siracusa, we gain so much more!" "But what do we gain?" asked his son. "My son, Siracusa, is the gateway to southern Sicily. All goods entering or leaving pass through this port." He leaned back and sighed. "Grapes, almonds, fruits, and wheat go out, while grains, oil, coal, kerosene, and iron come in." Salvatore sat quietly, and Francesco waited for him to respond. Nothing. "Alright, I'll explain it simply," Francesco said, and Salvatore felt the sting of the words. "What if we controlled the port? What if we extended our business to Siracusa?" Suddenly, Salvatore had an idea. "Protezione," he said. "Finally!" Francesco replied, mixing pride with disappointment. "Whoever controls the port controls commerce in the south. Imagine the money and power we could wield!" Salvatore understood his father's vision, but the execution of such a bold plan remained unclear.

Chapter 2:
A Pivotal Decision

Massimo Neri was finishing his early morning chores on his small farm in Almo, a tiny hamlet outside of Monterosso. He had fed the chickens, milked the cows, and all that was left was to mend a fence that separated his property from the neighboring one across the small brook that ran between them. Before getting to work on the fence, he decided to have a snack. Normally, his wife would prepare this, but she was away visiting a sick relative. In his kitchen, he made a meal consisting of a hunk of cheese, a ripe tomato, and a piece of hard salami. He poured himself a glass of fresh milk to complete the midday feast. Just as he sat down to enjoy his well-earned rest, he heard horses approaching up the steep path to the house. He went to the door and saw two men. He recognized one as Salvatore Arcuri, and a sense of dread washed over him. Salvatore dismounted and made his way to the porch while the other man remained on his horse. A barking dog was causing a commotion. Salvatore spoke up: "Il vostro cane mi sta infastidendo." (Your dog is bothering me.)

Before Massimo Neri could respond, Salvatore picked up a long-handled shovel that had been leaning against the porch and delivered two swift blows to the animal's head. The first blow made a sickening sound against the dog's skull, causing the animal to squeal in pain. It fell to its side, whimpering. Neri opened his door and was filled with rage. Before he could say or do anything, he saw the other man. He had a shotgun, and it was pointed directly at him. *The man was smiling.*

The second blow to the dog could be considered as merciful. It put the animal out of its misery.

"There. Now we can talk in peace without interruptions," hissed Salvatore. "I'm sorry. Did you want to tell me something?" Neri stood at the doorway, halfway in and halfway out. He felt as though his very life was at a halfway point as well; he might live, or he might not. This day had been inevitable. He was one of the few landowners in the Monterosso area who had refused to comply with "Il Leone." Today was his day of reckoning.

The funeral for Massimo Neri was simple, attended by his family, some friends and others from the tiny town. When Neri's wife returned to the farm, there was little left. The house, the outbuildings, the pasture were burned. The well was poisoned. The livestock slaughtered. The message was made clear, not only to the now widowed woman, but to any remaining recalcitrant landowners in the Monterosso region. Either do business with Il Leone, or deal with the consequences.

Vito Pedrotti was a busy man. He ran a profitable business selling fruit and vegetables in Naples—at least, that's what most people thought. In reality, Vito Pedrotti was the head of the largest crime family in southern Italy, excluding Sicily. From his home office located on Via Carlo Poerio, he oversaw operations involving protection, gambling, and prostitution across a wide area, and he certainly did not want to hear any bad news. One day, a young boy, around fourteen years old, burst into his office, barely kept in check by a burly bodyguard at the door. "What does he mean coming in here without an invitation?" the guard said as he held the skinny youngster by his upper arms. The lad comically tried to push past the guard, but the burly man could have easily restrained him if he wanted—or if Don Pedrotti commanded it. "Get him out of here," Pedrotti ordered. The situation was nearly resolved when the boy spoke up. "So, the great man doesn't want to hear about the very bad news from Almo?" The Don's expression changed; he was now curious. "Wait. Bring him here," he commanded. The boy was sweating profusely. "Give him some water," the Don instructed his guard. "Sit," he said firmly. The boy composed himself and began to tell the Don his story.

He and his parents had been in Monterossa, where they had relatives. While there, they heard about the murder of a farmer. "That's a nice story, but what on earth do I care about it?" The Don was clearly unhappy. "Perhaps you didn't know the name of the farmer," the boy said. "His name was Neri." Don Vito Pedrotti stared at the boy, now intrigued. "Neri, you say?" "Yes, Don. Massimo Neri. Isn't he related to your wife? If I'm wrong, I apologize a thousand times, and I will take my leave..." Massimo Neri was indeed someone the Don knew; he was the brother of Don Vito's wife. The boy then described the events leading up to the massacre at Almo. Don Vito was filled with anger. The bodyguard carefully observed his boss's face, recognizing a look he hadn't seen in many years. Pedrotti spoke: "Make sure he gets home safely." He then instructed the guard to return soon after. There was work to be done. Massimo Neri was indeed the brother of the wife of one of the most powerful men in southern Italy— the boss of bosses in Napoli. Even if it took a hundred years, vengeance would be sought. Don Vito Pedrotti had a veritable army he could call upon to carry out his unique brand of vengeance, and he would do just that.

Chapter 3:

Repercussions

Francesco Arcuri's decision to journey to the sun-drenched shores of Siracusa in October 1893 remains shrouded in mystery, a question that lingers in the minds of many. His son, Salvatore, wasn't altogether shocked by his father's bold move towards establishing connections in this unfamiliar land, but he felt a pang of disappointment that he would be excluded from the discussions. His father, known as Il Leone for his fierce determination and strength, would embark on this mission without him. "Why, why, why… the endless questions you pose," Francesco sighed, exasperation creeping into his voice as he faced his son. "Listen closely, Salvatore. What I am about to undertake is not only serious but fraught with danger. It's a path you are not yet ready to tread. Thus, I will assume this burden alone. What I will do is set the stage for our family's future. One day, this groundwork shall belong to you, for you and your descendants. The legacy I forge will endure, passed down through the generations of Arcuris yet to come." Francesco Arcuri—deliberate and meticulous—had already made initial overtures to influential officials in Siracusa. He believed that finalizing these negotiations would merely require his determination and strategic savvy. With his keen sense of business, he was convinced that a well-timed quid pro quo would grant him access to the thriving import markets. Soon, he envisioned himself imposing his will on the local merchants, who he perceived as overly confident in their control of the bustling Siracusian port. Thus, Il Leone would secure not just wealth but also a formidable legacy for his family.

Meanwhile, in the gritty streets of Napoli, Dominick Pavero navigated the underbelly of the city with a reputation already cemented by blood. At the tender age of 29, he was considered a "made man" within the revered Mafia ranks—untouchable by virtue of his deeds. Having committed murder at the direct orders of his boss, he enjoyed a precarious form of protection; to harm him would invoke a violent retaliation from those who understood the unspoken rules of their world. Pavero was a soldier, or "soldato," in the formidable Pedrotti family. With twenty lives extinguished at the behest of Don Pedrotti, he wore his experiences like a badge of honor, never taking a life without explicit command. When summoned to the opulent yet intimidating residence of Don Pedrotti, he understood the unwritten possibility that he might be given yet another task that could alter the course of someone's life—perhaps even his own. Physically, Dominick Pavero was an imposing figure: he had thick, curly hair that framed a broad, muscular neck, and his robust frame resembled that of a fireplug—solid and unyielding. His arms, reminiscent of a blacksmith's, showcased formidable musculature, hinting at strength forged through hard labor. A distinctive tattoo adorned his right bicep, a mark that spoke of his loyalties and past. Despite his powerful stature, he walked with a subtle limp, the result of being born with a right leg just slightly shorter than his left. His voice, unexpectedly high-pitched for such a physically imposing man, often left those in his presence taken aback. Few survived the consequences of mocking Dominick; a severe beating was a very real possibility for anyone who dared to insult him.

"Dominick, would you care for a drink?" the Don offered, his deep voice resonating with authority. "No, thank you, Don," he replied, a hint of respect evident in his tone. "Good boy. I never trust anyone who drinks before midday," Pedrotti proclaimed, his eyes glinting as he lit a Toscany cigar, the flame flickering momentarily against the shadows of the room. As he blew out the match, fragrant tendrils of smoke swirled and danced around his head, creating an almost mystical aura. The sunlight streaming through the window behind him cast a celestial glow, illuminating the great man in a way that made him seem larger than life. Dominick found himself captivated, his admiration for the Don flowing like an unstoppable tide; there was nothing he wouldn't do for him. "Dominick, I have a particularly important job for you," the Don continued, his tone shifting to one of gravity. "You're aware that my brother-in-law was murdered a few weeks ago in Almo... you knew that, didn't you?" Dominick nodded, his heart pounding with a mix of intrigue and trepidation. "It would be my greatest honor to carry out this duty, sir." He took a deep breath to steady himself. "When? Where?" The Don leaned forward slightly, his expression serious. "Siracusa. October eighth."

The Mafia, particularly the notorious Sicilian Mafia, emerged in the tumultuous landscape of 19th-century Sicily. It was an enigmatic and loosely knit association of criminal factions, each with its own hierarchy and a shared, unwritten code of conduct that governed their illicit activities. At the heart of this underworld were "families," known locally as "clans" or "cosche," each claiming dominion over a specific territory— be it a quaint village, a bustling town, or a gritty neighborhood (Borgata) within a sprawling city. Within their domain, these families operated an array of rackets, ensuring that their influence was felt at every level. Members proudly referred to themselves as "men of honor," while the outside world labeled them simply as Mafiosi, whispered in tones of both fear and fascination. The term "mafia" itself springs from the Sicilian word "mafiusu" (in Italian, "mafioso"), a term that conveys a sense of swagger but also translates to boldness and bravado—traits that are vital for survival in their perilous realm. According to those who defected from its ranks (the pentiti), the true name of the Mafia is "Cosa Nostra," or "Our Thing," a phrase that encapsulates their insular and fiercely protective code. Recruiting outsiders is rare within the Mafia's shadowy operations, as such individuals are seen as vulnerabilities—expendable liabilities—and often meet grim fates soon after their initial involvement. The violence that permeates the Mafia is predominantly directed at rival families vying for power, territory, and lucrative business dealings. In Sicily, this brutal reality is exacerbated by the presence of numerous smaller families, leading to an atmosphere fraught with tension and conflict. When a loved one is murdered, a vendetta is often ignited, sparking a cycle of retribution that can engulf entire communities. The Mafia wields its power through a chilling reputation for ruthlessness, capable of committing acts of violence, even murder, against anyone who dares to cross them. This fearsome reputation acts as a formidable deterrent, allowing mafiosi to protect their clients from afar, functioning as the unseen guardians of their interests. In this precarious balance, a mafioso's reputation is paramount; unlike in other professions, there is no middle ground. He is perceived as either a stalwart protector or a complete failure. The stakes are incredibly high, as a single misstep can lead to catastrophic consequences—a failed act of protection can shatter a mafioso's reputation and, with it, his livelihood. For Don Vito Pedrotti of Napoli, the loss of his brother-in-law was a wound that demanded retribution—a wound that could never heal until Massimo Neri's death was avenged. Through an intricate web of informants, Don Pedrotti pieced together the grim puzzle surrounding the murder. He discovered that a member of the Arcuri crime family, a loosely organized yet dangerous faction, was responsible for his brother-in-law's demise. In his quest for justice, irony dripped from an unexpected source: a local public official from Modica, situated just south of Ragusa. This man, driven by his own motives, had no loyalty to Francesco Arcuri and used the chaos of the situation to share invaluable information. When questioned about the incident, he unveiled the sordid details of the murder and named those behind the sinister order, each revelation bringing Don Pedrotti one step closer to the vengeance he sought.

Dominick Pavero awoke early on the morning of October 7th. It was a Thursday, and he had arrived in Siracusa a day earlier. The distance from Naples to Siracusa was more than 600 km. His journey had begun on Monday, with the Don arranging every detail, from false identity papers to a disguise that included a suit and advice on growing a mustache. The long journey took him along the coast, past Amalfi and Sorrento—two towns he had heard of but never seen. A tour of these beautiful seaside towns would have to wait until the job was completed. The train was comfortable for the most part, but it felt like it would never end. Among the scheduled stops were Salerno, Totora, and finally Reggio, at the toe of Italy. From there, he crossed the strait of Messina and traveled along the coast of the Gulf of Catania toward Siracusa, which is at the southeast end of Sicily. There, a man named Michaelantonio was waiting for him. Michaelantonio was tall, very thin, and gaunt. Dominick thought he looked like he owned a funeral parlor, which, in fact, he did. This grim figure was to make the "final arrangements" for a hit, an irony that Dominick couldn't help but acknowledge. MichaelAntonio led Dominick to his carriage and asked if he needed anything. "Just a bath, some food, and some rest," Dominick replied. "Arrangements have been made," the gaunt man responded. "Also, I have a package for you from our friend." Dominick understood exactly what the man meant by "package." Since he had been expressly told not to bring any "tools" (weapons), he was certain that the tools he would need were waiting for him in Siracusa. The carriage turned onto a street that Dominick recognized by the sign on the stucco building at the corner. It read "Via Pitia." "Here we are," said the gaunt man. "This is your home for as long as it takes for you to..." He caught himself mid-sentence. "Until I complete the job?" Dominick finished for him. "Er, yes... your job, by all means!" MichaelAntonio stuttered. The building on Via Pitia served as both the residence and the business of the gaunt man. On the first floor was the "Michaelantonio Gibenza Funeral Parlor," and upstairs was the home where he lived with his wife and four children. After perfunctory greetings from Mrs. Gibenza and three of the children, Dominick was led upstairs to his room. Mrs. Gibenza was told that Dominick was a coffin salesman. He chuckled to himself and asked where he might clean up. The bath did him good, and the meal prepared by Mrs. Gibenza was delicious. Dominick enjoyed Sicilian delicacies, such as Panelle, a kind of fried chickpea fritter, and a simple but delicious coastal favorite: pasta with sardines. He closed his eyes and savored every bite, enjoying the best finocchio (wild fennel) he had ever tasted. As if that were not enough, Mrs. Gibenza's daughter brought out a tray of "sfingi," Sicilian carnival donuts.

A steaming cup of espresso and a brief discussion about coffins rounded out Dominick's evening. He excused himself, thanked the hostess profusely, and retired to his room. It was eleven o'clock on Wednesday, October 7th. Francesco Arcuri had less than twelve hours to live. Once inside his room, Dominick heard a light knock at his door. In the hallway stood Maria, the daughter who served the donuts. She curtsied; her eyes cast downward and handed him a package. "This is for you. My father asked me to bring it to you." "Thank you," Dominick whispered. "Sei il benvenuto e buona notte," Maria replied with a smile. Dominick locked the door and placed the package on the bed. It was thirty centimeters long and about ten centimeters thick, wrapped in brown paper and secured with butcher's string. He carefully unwrapped it, revealing his tools. Among them, he immediately spotted a revolver—a Bodeo, a real beauty. This

Italian service revolver was used by the Army. Solidly constructed, it was a six-shot model. Dominick, knowledgeable about firearms, recognized it as the version produced for non-commissioned officers. It had been freshly oiled and was in excellent condition.

The gun measured approximately 18 centimeters in length, including the barrel, making it lethal enough for the task at hand. The cartridges were 10.35 Ordinanza Italiana shells, which Dominick approved of. Included with the gun were a folding knife and a small, hand-drawn map containing instructions. The map indicated an address: "4 Via Tisia." According to the gaunt man, Via Tisia was about two blocks from the funeral parlor. The building was a public structure, housing offices for various professionals in Siracusa. It was no more than a five-minute walk from Via Pitia. Dominick immediately left the house and walked to #4 Via Tisia, timing the walk—it took him four minutes. According to the intelligence available to Don Pedrotti, Francesco Arcuri was scheduled to meet with several men at 10 o'clock in the morning on October 8th inside the building on Via Tisia. Outside the building, there was a directory listing various names, including that of Vincenzo Artelli, "Avvocato - beni immobili," or lawyer specializing in real estate. At exactly 8:45 AM on October 8th, Dominick woke up and dressed in the white jacket and pants he had brought with him. He studied his reflection in the mirror; the white suit made him appear official, like a delivery man. The matching white cap completed the look. His mustache rendered him almost unrecognizable, even to himself. He tucked the knife into his sock and placed the loaded gun in the small of his back, under his jacket. After having breakfast, he left the house on Via Pitia at 9:15. Francesco Arcuri would be dead within fifty minutes, but first, Dominick made a stop at the florist shop located halfway between the gaunt man's home and the scene of the crime. When Dominick opened the shop door, the bell clanged loudly. The floral shop, simply identified by the sign in the window as

"Fiori per Angelina," was small and tidy. From behind the counter, the proprietor greeted him. "Buongiorno. E come posso aiutarla?" Dominick ordered a modest bouquet of roses, paid for them, and left the shop. It was 9:40.

He stood on the walkway across from #4 Via Tisia, observing the bustling scene around him. People went about their daily activities, and horse-drawn wagons clacked along the cobbled streets. A street cleaner was sweeping up after the horses while a man extinguished the gas streetlamps. Shopkeepers began to unfurl their awnings and open their businesses for the day. "Via Tisia is busier than I thought," Dominick mused to himself as he mentally prepared for the task ahead. He planned to wait until the target was inside the office of Vincenzo Artelli, the lawyer. Under the pretense of delivering a bouquet, he would make his way to the office and assassinate the man responsible for Massimo Neri's death. At 9:53, a carriage pulled up in front of #4. Out stepped Francesco Arcuri, the Don, known as "Il Leone." Dominick sized him up, noting that he was accompanied by a bodyguard—an expected precaution but hardly something Dominick Pavero couldn't handle. Two minutes after watching Il Leone and his companion enter the building, Dominick walked in himself. No one stopped him, but as he started toward the stairs, he encountered a man who appeared to be a custodian. "What is your business?" the man asked. "I have a delivery of beautiful flowers for Signor Artelli from his wife. I believe it may be his birthday," Dominick replied, pleased with his performance. His Sicilian accent was on point. The man pointed toward the stairs. "Un volo in alto." Dominick ascended the steps, forcing himself to slow down and breathe deeply. He felt the weight of the gun tucked behind him and the blade strapped to his ankle, with beads of sweat beginning to form around his temples. At the landing, he overheard voices—two men greeting each other. One was the lawyer, and the other was his target. The third voice belonged to Giuseppe

Ruggiero, a soldier in the Arcuri family. Don Pedrotti's intelligence was commendable; if Arcuri had brought "muscle," it would likely be Ruggiero. Dominick knew Ruggiero carried a handgun and that he was left-handed—information that could prove crucial. Dominick reached the office door at exactly 10:03 a.m. He knocked, and just as his fist made contact, the door, which was slightly ajar, swung open.

As it swung open, he saw Sr. Artelli seated behind a large wooden desk. Seated in the chair before the desk, Arcuri. Standing off to the right side, the bodyguard. Dominick smiled. The lawyer looked annoyed. He asked, *"What can we do for you?"*

In his mind, Dominick answered, *"You can all die."*

Dominick's instincts, honed for more than ten years kicked in. "I have a delivery for you", he stated.

"What is it, from who?"

These were the last words out of the mouth of the lawyer. *There were no words uttered by either Arcuri or Ruggiero.*

Dominick took several strides into the small room but toward the hulking bodyguard. For a moment, Dominick saw a look of suspicion in the eyes of Giuseppe Ruggiero. Perhaps his instinct was that of a killer recognizing another killer. In a flash, Dominick produced the Bodeo. The first shot hit Giuseppe Ruggiero in the right temple. His eyes rolled back in his head, and he dropped to his knees, dead before hitting the floor with his face.

Dominick turned his attention to the lawyer, who was still seated, stunned by the actions of the *floral deliveryman*. Dominick was a mere meter away and to the side. He aimed the revolver and fired point blank into his temple. There was a "whoosh" of blood and gray matter exiting from the opposite side of Vincenzo Artelli. His body became limp, and he slumped and slid to the floor.

The look in the eyes of Don Francesco Arcuri, Boss of Bosses from Ragusa Sicily, the man widely known as "Il Leone", was a mixture of *recognition, fear, defiance and defeat.*

Dominick dramatically announced:

"Oggi morirai per i tuoi peccati contro don Pedrotti."

"Today, you will die for the sins committed against Don Pedrotti".

For "Il Leone", Dominick saved the six-inch blade. He swiftly dispatched the man of honor with a deft cut across his throat. As Arcuri struggled to breathe, Dominick dispatched him with a single gunshot into his left eye.

Dominick threw the bouquet across the dead body of Don Arcuri. He looked at his pocket watch. It was 10: 12 a.m.

Chapter 4:

Vendetta

The news of Don Francesco Salvatore Arcuri's death reverberated through the cobblestone streets of Ragusa like a thunderclap, leaving the residents in shock. The Don had been a longstanding figure in the community, a familiar presence for decades, and now he was gone at the relatively young age of 46. Whispers and speculations spread through the town like wildfire, often far more sensational than the truth. While some locals claimed that an enraged husband had caught the Don with a lady friend, others suggested that he had fallen afoul of the Mafia, unable to pay back his debts. The grim reality, however, was that his assassination stemmed from actions taken by his eldest son.

The brutal murder of Massimo Neri had set off a chain of events that culminated in the paradoxical and tragic demise of the esteemed man, Il Leone. As two elderly men stood in the bustling town square, one remarked, "We will surely not see his like again in our lifetime," nostalgia thick in his voice. His companion, however, replied with a note of worry, "We may be in for worse times." His eyes darkened as he considered the impending future now in the hands of a barely twenty-five-year-old man-child, Salvatore Arcuri, whom some had dubbed the "young lion." The townsfolk were engulfed in a storm of mixed emotions; on one hand, they hoped the iron-fisted control of the father would dissipate.

On the other, they feared that the son might prove to be an even greater tyrant. "He has a terrible temper," said the man who owned a modest livery service, casting furtive glances around as he spoke. "From what I hear, his reckless actions got the father killed." He spoke in hushed tones, acutely aware that voicing such thoughts about an Arcuri could invite trouble. Little did the shopkeepers and citizens of Ragusa realize that Salvatore Arcuri would soon face challenges far beyond their expectations. A hastily convened meeting called by Underboss Giuseppe Garfagnini was set to occur in a discreet location on the outskirts of Ragusa, far removed from prying eyes and ears. "Well, here we are, cowering in the dark like frightened children," Giuseppe remarked, his weary voice echoing in the shadowy room. Salvatore was the last to enter, and the weight of his presence was palpable as everyone turned to gaze at him. Garfagnini, thin and bald, was the oldest member of the Arcuri family, nearing seventy, and he exuded an air of resignation, keenly aware of the storm brewing ahead. "You all know what comes next, don't you?" he pressed, his voice tinged with anxiety as he referenced the perceived vulnerability of the Arcuri family after the loss of its patriarch. "They'll come at us from all angles," he added, his words steeped in foreboding, signaling the impending chaos that was likely to unfold.

"Let them come," barked soldier Vincent Zanetti. He felt he should have accompanied the boss on his business trip to Siracusa. "None of this would have happened if I were with the Don, and you know it." Spit flew from his mouth as he spoke. "Lower your voice, for God's sake, Vincent," implored Garfagnini. "We all know your prowess, but what's done is done." Frank Nicastro, the lowest-ranking soldier, spoke next. "Yes, and we know why the Don decided to leave you behind, don't we?" Nicastro insinuated that Vincent Zanetti's lack of sobriety was the reason the Don chose the younger Ruggiero to accompany him. "Why, you bastard..." huffed Zanetti. "I ought to..." He couldn't complete his sentence. "Silence, all of you!" demanded Salvatore Arcuri. "What a spectacle this is." "Fact: my father is dead, as is Giuseppe Ruggiero." The room fell deadly silent. "Another fact: we can expect our enemies to take advantage of what is happening here and now," he continued. "This discord will destroy us." The six remaining members of the Arcuri family agreed. It wouldn't be long before they were forced to fight for what they had, including their lives. Instructions were given to the men, with one immediate concern being the protection of certain family members, as there was a real possibility that vengeance might extend to the so-called innocents. With assignments in hand, the men split up. One thing they could all agree on was that their criminal enterprise was fading fast unless bold action was taken. As the new boss, Salvatore Arcuri had to make the most critical decision of his young life—one that would affect everyone he knew. What Salvatore had imagined was clarified during the meeting. The binding force of the Arcuri family had been his father, Francesco, known as "Il Leone."

Salvatore had no doubt that he could not keep the family from imploding. He arrived at his decision surprisingly quickly. He knew that his actions had created this catastrophe and that his life was in imminent danger. Each of the remaining members of the Arcuri crime family sensed that the assassination of their leader would not be an ending but rather the beginning of more wrenching changes. Although their initial suspicion regarding a takeover of the Arcuri territory was correct, they misjudged where the enemy would come from. Each man, experienced in the life they had chosen, recognized that they were in a perilous situation—one that could affect not only them but also their families.

The Arcuri territory stretched from Enna in the north to Pozzallo on the southern coast. Its western boundary was near Gela, and its eastern boundary reached Palazzolo, about 75 km west of Siracusa. Don Arcuri wanted to extend the eastern boundary to include the coastal port of Siracusa so he could control shipping in and out of this important entry point to southern Sicily. Underboss Garfagnini and his men, Frank Nicastro and Tomaso Contorno, believed that a neighboring family might try to take over. The powerful Caltanissetta family had long wanted the Ragusa area to expand their interests. Don Mario Mussomeli, the head of the family, made his plans clear. In the past, there were several small battles, especially around the village of Riesi. The Arcuris pushed back the invasion, with help from an unexpected ally, Don Rico Misilmeri. He led the most powerful gang in Sicily and likely wanted the Ragusa territory for himself. Like Francesco Arcuri, he was also eyeing the port of Siracusa. Misilmeri stepped in during the troubles in Riesi and used his influence to resolve the conflict. However, no one expected that the takeover of the Ragusa region would come from the mainland of Italy. Don Vito Pedrotti of Naples was making plans for that. Vito Paolo Pedrotti was born in 1839 in Castellammare, a town in northwestern Sicily. He was born to peasant parents and had a rough childhood. At sixteen, he joined a gang. By thirty, he had become a recognized man in the criminal world. Seeking better opportunities in southern Italy, he and his allies took control of Naples by the time he was thirty-five. They built a criminal empire there, controlling the port and various illegal activities, such as gambling and prostitution, while also providing protection. By 1875, Pedrotti was richer and more powerful than anyone else in Italy. He ran his operations openly from a storefront that sold wholesale fruit and vegetables on busy Via Carlo Poerlo.

Like any astute, albeit ruthless businessman, Don Vito Pedrotti eliminated competition, controlled judges and law enforcement, and wielded the threat of violence with remarkable efficiency. Additionally, he was always looking to expand his empire, which led to the bold decision to cross the Golfo di Noto and seize control of the port city of Siracusa. He understood that such a move would be fraught with danger, but he believed it was a gamble worth taking. Pedrotti commanded a virtual army of nearly one hundred men, far outnumbering the relatively small Arcuri family. His plan involved sending fifty of these men into the Siracusa area over a two-week period to eliminate any officials who might obstruct his path. His ruthless nature made him confident in the feasibility of this scheme. A week prior, he planned to send twenty men to Ragusa to kidnap Salvatore Arcuri. The Pedrottis would then pressure the remaining members of the Arcuri family to surrender their holdings in southeastern Sicily and renounce any ambitions they had for Siracusa. The ultimate insurance policy would be to kill Salvatore if necessary. The plan was well-developed and ready for implementation, with the key objective being the kidnapping and murder of the son of "Il Leone."

Chapter 5:

Fateful Decision

Salvatore Arcuri had always trusted his instincts. Following his gut feelings often helped him succeed and stay alive. Now, in his early twenties, he faced his biggest decision yet: he would disappear. No one—his mother, siblings, or anyone in the criminal organization—would know what happened to him. Part of Salvatore wanted to stay and fight for what his father had built. However, his instincts told him he needed to survive to fight another day, and to do that, he had to flee. He worried about what Il Leone would think. Would his father be ashamed of him for running away, or would he support his decision to save himself and possibly create a new empire? Salvatore had always resented his father's strict control and his "do things my way" attitude. This reasoning helped Salvatore justify his big decision. He planned to finalize his escape soon and would tell only one person: Underboss Giuseppe Garfagnini. Even Giuseppe would not know where Salvatore would go. Garfagnini was from an older generation—old enough to be Salvatore's grandfather. Salvatore respected him and considered him like family. He felt Giuseppe could help watch over his mother and immediate family. Even though he thought they would be safe, he wanted to ensure their protection. In the old Mafia, certain rules kept innocent family members safe. Getting Giuseppe's promise could only help. Salvatore's view was naïve. By the 1890s, many old rules of the Sicilian gangs were disappearing. A new generation of criminals often ignored what they saw as outdated customs. Giuseppe, the rest of the Arcuri gang, and Salvatore's family were not guaranteed safety as the Pedrotti plan unfolded. Salvatore knew he had less than a week to disappear. He quietly developed a plan that included where to go, how to travel, and an uncertain future. Salvatore's instincts led him to find a place where he could live anonymously for an unknown time: Campania, specifically Benevento. He targeted several small hamlets in that area; the smaller, the better.

The journey ahead loomed long and arduous, a daunting prospect that filled Giuseppe Garfagnini with both anticipation and trepidation. Armed with meticulous calculations, he knew he would traverse the strait and travel into the heart of Italy, covering a sprawling distance of approximately 700 kilometers. While that figure appeared manageable on a map, in his mind, it felt like traversing a million miles. Saturday mornings for Giuseppe followed a comforting routine, a rhythm he had embraced for years. He awakened at the break of dawn, the soft glow of sunlight filtering through the curtains. After splashing his face with cool water, he meticulously shaved and combed his thinning gray hair, casting a critical eye at his reflection. He dressed carefully in woolen trousers and a flannel shirt, layering a silken vest over his frame. His well-worn suit jacket hung patiently on a nail by the kitchen door, awaiting the occasion to be worn. As he ambled into the kitchen, his wife of forty-three years greeted him with a warm smile, her presence a source of comfort. The aromatic scent of freshly brewed espresso filled the air, mingling with the sweet fragrance of a brioche col tupo that sat invitingly on the table, lovingly prepared by her hands. "And what is on your agenda today, my husband?" she asked, her voice laced with genuine curiosity. "I thought we had fresh figs," he replied, his mind still clouded by sleep. "No, we gave several away to my sister when she visited. Would you like some Pasticceria instead?" she offered, her tone cheerful. "Pasticceria? You know how I feel about that," he retorted, an edge of frustration creeping into his voice. She brushed off his complaint with practiced ease, focusing instead on her morning rituals. "So where are you going, or must I ask you ten times?" she pressed, concern edging into her voice. With a deep breath, Giuseppe bit into the soft, flaky brioche and savored the moment, letting the rich flavor mingle with the bold espresso as he slowly sipped from his cup, the world outside awaiting his next move.

"I have some business that will take me into town this morning," he explained dismissively. Giuseppe did have important business in town, but he was sworn to secrecy by Salvatore Arcuri and could not disclose any details of the meeting. Giuseppe Garfagnini, the man Salvatore was to trust with his mother's life, was about to leave for Castelluccio, a forty-five-minute wagon ride away. It was a journey Giuseppe had made more times than he could count but today would be his last ride. He finished his espresso, put on his jacket and hat, and kissed his wife. Salvatore glanced at his pocket watch. It was past eight o'clock, and Giuseppe was late. He waited another thirty minutes, his mind racing with worry as he considered the risks of waiting in Castelluccio. With each passing minute, his restlessness grew. At nine o'clock, he decided to leave. He wondered if Giuseppe had been delayed for a good reason, changed his mind about meeting, or if something had happened to his friend. Regardless, he knew that any further delay could be a mistake—and possibly a fatal one. Salvatore decided to ride toward Giuseppe's homestead. Perhaps the wagon had encountered an issue, like a broken wheel on the unforgiving dirt road. He urged his horse into a gallop. By nine-forty, he reached the halfway point between Castelluccio and Giuseppe's place. It was at a bend in the road that he made a horrifying discovery: there was a wagon, and the horse was grazing nearby. Dismounting cautiously with his shotgun at his side, Salvatore tied his horse and then saw Giuseppe's lifeless body hanging from the branch of an oak tree. Looking around and seeing no one else, Salvatore managed to cut Giuseppe down, lowering his limp body to the ground. Who could have done this? Or had Giuseppe taken his own life? Regardless, Salvatore knew that his plans had to be adjusted. The first part of his plan was ruined.

Chapter 6:
Harsh Reality

With the only person he truly trusted dead, Salvatore had to face the harsh reality of his situation. How or why Giuseppe died was just as important as figuring out what to do next. Without anyone else he could trust, Salvatore's mother and siblings were at risk of becoming targets for the vendetta squad. As much as he wanted to believe in the code that traditionally protected innocent loved ones from retribution, he knew the harsh truth: times were changing. After burying his underboss and freeing his horse, Salvatore mounted it and rode to Giuseppe's home, located about twenty minutes away. Even from a kilometer away, he could detect the acrid smell of smoke wafting from the fireplace of the Garfagnini homestead. The house itself was a modest stucco building with a red clay tile roof, situated on approximately seven hectares of land at the junction of two small roads near the village of San Giocomo. Upon arrival, he was greeted by an eerie silence. Everything seemed in order, yet he felt that something was amiss. About fifty meters from the farmhouse, Salvatore dismounted, tied his horse to a tree, grabbed his shotgun, and carefully surveyed his surroundings before walking slowly toward the building. As he approached, he could hear chickens cackling from the rear of the property. He saw no outward signs of trouble, and yet… With his shotgun ready, he reached the front door—a grayish, weather-worn wooden door that was slightly ajar. Salvatore held his weapon firmly, with his right index finger on the trigger and his left hand around the barrel. He nudged the door open with his left foot, and it creaked inward into the darkened kitchen. He entered cautiously, surveying the room; there was nothing to see. It appeared that someone had been preparing a meal, as there was food on the table, a jug of wine, and two glasses. Salvatore walked slowly toward the bedroom. The small bed was made, and nothing seemed out of place. Convinced that there was nothing unusual inside the house, Salvatore exited and made his way toward the barn, which was about ten meters from the house. He passed the chickens and the enclosure where the cows were grazing before entering the barn. It was there that Salvatore Arcuri realized his instincts were correct. The bodies of Giuseppe's wife and an unidentified man—possibly a laborer—were hanging by their necks. A shiver ran down his spine. He felt a surge of revulsion, anger, and fear all at once. He now understood that his own family was in grave danger. Whoever was behind this act was both vicious and merciless. While he could comprehend the killing of the underboss, the murder of innocents made no sense at all.

    Salvatore's head was spinning as his horse galloped away from San Giocomo, moving as swiftly as possible toward Avola, a coastal town south of Siracusa. There, he would meet an ally who would help him escape Sicily and navigate his uncertain future in Italy. Aldo Butera understood that he would one day owe a favor to Don Arcuri, stemming from a favor he had received from the Don long ago. This quid pro quo was an unspoken agreement that everyone clearly understood. The Don's previous intervention on Aldo Butera's behalf came with this expectation. For a simple man like Aldo, there were no questions to ask; he instinctively knew that this day would eventually arrive. Aldo held an important position at the docks of Avola, where he had enough authority and influence to arrange discreet travel when necessary. Soon, he would be called upon to repay his debt to the Arcuri family. In his role, he was prepared to provide safe passage for the son of Il Leone. Reggio di Calabria lies at the very toe of the Italian peninsula. From there, Salvatore would be on his own to reach a secret destination known to no one, for obvious reasons. Salvatore needed to go somewhere he had never been, a place so remote that it would be nearly impossible for his enemies to find him. In his bag, he carried a revolver, a knife, some clothes, his Miraculous Medal, some currency, and a crumbled old map of southern central Italy. The last official act of Giuseppe Garfagnini was to arrange for Salvatore to meet his contact. Fortunately for Salvatore, the old man managed to make these arrangements before meeting his fate. Salvatore arrived at the port at midnight. His instructions were to find "Vis Piccione," number 32, and ask for Aldo Butera. Aldo Butera was a slight man, short in stature, with gray hair and wearing eyeglasses. He appeared to be about fifty years old. Before Salvatore could say a word, the older man greeted him. "Il Leone, I presume?" No one ever referred to Salvatore by his father's title. "I am Salvatore," he corrected gently. "I knew your father many years ago," Aldo said. "You look just like him. Please, come inside." Salvatore hurried into the modest stucco home. It was clear that the space functioned both as a residence and a place of business. From this location, travelers could arrange transport by steamships, rowboats, and everything in between. Aldo's name had been mentioned many times by Salvatore's father; they had been friends for a long time.

"First, please allow me to express my deepest condolences to you and, of course, your family," he said, his voice filled with genuine warmth. "I am certain your father shared stories of our adventures and our longstanding friendship. I am here to assist you during this difficult time." Salvatore felt a warmth in his chest from the man's sincerity, yet a heavy weariness hung over him. His stomach grumbled with hunger, and a wave of fear coursed through him. Trust was a fragile thing, and he wasn't sure whom he could rely on anymore. "Thank you, and yes, he spoke highly of you, Mr. Butera. For now, I need transit papers, a bath, and a meal, if that's possible," he replied, his voice barely above a whisper. Aldo, with his practiced efficiency, had already prepared the letters of transit, and he carried a satchel bursting with clothing, toiletries, a few intriguing books, and a significant amount of lire—far more than Salvatore had anticipated. Mr. Butera led him to a cozy, private room adorned with soft lighting and modest furnishings, then swiftly returned with a tray laden with food: a generous portion of steaming pasta, a slice of fresh bread, a glass of deep red wine, and a cold jug of water, all arranged with care. "If you don't mind, I have arranged your passage for six o'clock in the morning. Leaving at that early hour will be much safer," Butera reassured him, his tone steady and calm. Salvatore felt a sense of urgency but was in no position to negotiate the departure time. "Good. I will be ready to leave then. Thank you," he intoned, trying to mask the turmoil churning inside him. As night fell, Salvatore tossed and turned in his unfamiliar surroundings. The bedding felt as hard as stone beneath him, yet it was the gravity of the life-altering decision he had made that robbed him of sleep. In less than six hours, Salvatore Arcuri would embark on a journey that could forever alter his fate. Behind him lay an uncertain future, heavy with the worry for his mother and two siblings, whose lives he was leaving behind amid shadows of doubt and longing.

Chapter 7:
Journey to Campania

Salvatore responded suddenly to the light rapping on his bedroom door. He had only managed to sleep fitfully for a very brief period after retiring a little past midnight. It was likely around five-thirty. He heard a man whisper: "Partiremo a breve, amico Mio. Ho preparato qualcosa per te da mangiare" ("We will leave shortly my friend. I have prepared something for you to eat.") It was Aldo. It was time to leave. Salvatore hurried through his morning routine, splashing water on his face, putting on the clothes provided by his host, and grabbing his satchel containing all his worldly possessions. The sun had yet to rise. The wagon ride was bumpy, and Aldo apologized. "We will be there soon," he promised. They reached the dock in a short time. During the ride, Salvatore saw hardly anyone on the road. This suited him just fine. The fewer people who saw him, the better, and the fewer who knew where he was ultimately going, the safer he felt. Aldo spoke little, and aside from the sounds of the horses and the wagon's wheels on the rough road, Salvatore only heard gulls in the distant darkness. In truth, even Salvatore was unaware of his destination. He dared not reveal this information to anyone—not to family members, business associates, or even Aldo Butera. Aldo, for his part, knew better than to ask. As they finalized certain details regarding the trip, Aldo Butera simply said, "Dio vi benedica nel vostro viaggio." Salvatore kissed Aldo on both cheeks and thanked him. The boat that was to take Salvatore to his destination was loaded with vegetables, bound for Reggio di Calabria. The journey across the strait was quick and efficient. Along with Salvatore, there were maybe six other men, all dressed in work clothes. Salvatore was dressed to look like these men who loaded and unloaded the boat at the docks. The other men may have speculated among themselves about the identity of their passenger on this trip, but they knew enough not to voice their suspicions aloud. The captain, a grizzled veteran of many such trips, was a man of few words. He also understood the value of discretion, having been well-paid to transport the stranger quietly and efficiently. Soon enough, the port of Reggio di Calabria became visible through the light fog, which began to lift as the sun rose over the southern Italian port. The stevedores were busy at work, loading and unloading a variety of ships of different sizes at the bustling facility. Salvatore was impressed by what was essentially just a mid-sized port. "What must the port of Naples be like?" he wondered.

Salvatore grabbed his satchel and disembarked, facing a decision that he had not fully settled upon: Where would he end up? He found a café near the main dock and ordered a cup of espresso. Reaching inside his jacket, Salvatore produced the well-worn map of southern Italy that he always referred to. "Mezzogiorno" was a broad area, consisting of the lands south of Rome. Traditionally poorer, less educated, and often looked down upon by the wealthier, more industrialized northern Italians, southern Italy reminded Salvatore of his native Sicily; here, he felt at home. As he studied his map, Salvatore quickly oriented himself. Reggio di Calabria was located at the toe of Italy's boot, on the southwest coast. He traced his right index finger along the path leading northward, above the great port city of Naples, but inland, toward the central section, away from the coast. This region, known as Benevento, was rural, isolated, yet not too far from either the port of Naples or the Adriatic Sea. While examining the map, he came across a series of tiny towns within the region. "I must become invisible," he reminded himself. In the heart of that area, in fact, in the middle of south-central Italy, lay his future home. Within the Campania-Benevento region, equally distant from Naples to the west and the ports along the Adriatic Sea, was the village of Foiano di Val Fortore. When he asked several people about Foiano and its distance from Reggio, he was met with blank stares; no one seemed to know where this place was. This further convinced Salvatore that this isolated village in the heart of Italy was the perfect location for him to hide, reflect, and begin a new life.

The journey northward to Benevento loomed ahead, a long and arduous expedition that would stretch over approximately 600 kilometers. Salvatore found himself contemplating the unknowns of the road: the condition of the paths ahead, the rugged terrain, and the potential threat of bandits lurking in shadowy corners. He was uncertain about the availability of crucial resources—food, water, and shelter—but despite these uncertainties, he felt a flicker of determination. He invested in a sturdy horse, an old but reliable saddle, and some well-worn bedding. As he prepared for the trek, he filled his pack with dried figs, rustic bread, and a canteen brimming with fresh water. Along with these essentials, he carried a gun, a sharp knife, some currency, and a map marked with careful strokes. Only one thing remained to complete his preparations: a new identity. Though he believed that the name "Arcuri" might go unnoticed in the remote expanses of the countryside, memories of his father's teachings resurfaced. Il Leone, a man of wisdom, often conveyed lessons through parables that intrigued young Salvatore, deeply embedding their meanings in his mind. One particular lesson about preparation resonated fiercely—a lesson learned while constructing a humble chicken coop. As his father meticulously assembled the pieces of wood, he instructed Salvatore to measure and cut the boards. Eager to impress, the boy took up the crosscut saw, beaming as he presented a freshly cut board to his father. Yet, disappointment loomed as Il Leone examined the offering; the board was cut a full inch too short, rendering it useless. With a steady gaze, Il Leone imparted a lesson that would echo through time: "Misurare due volte, tagliare una volta," he said resolutely. The words translated to, "Measure twice, cut once." This valuable lesson left an indelible mark on Salvatore, teaching him that in tasks requiring meticulous precision, proper preparation is the key to success. Failure to prepare could lead to dire consequences. Thus, Salvatore resolved to reluctantly adopt a new name. As he journeyed along the winding road from Reggio di Calabria toward his soon-to-be new home, he spotted a signpost that read,

"Teggiano, 10 km." At that pivotal moment, halfway through his journey, Salvatore Arcuri transformed into Salvatore Teggiano. He crafted a cover story about his identity and his reasons for traveling to this region, claiming he was orphaned, had no family ties, and was departing his southern home in search of new opportunities. As October nights fell, they brought a chill that seeped into the marrow, with temperatures plunging to a bitter one or two degrees Celsius. In the higher elevations, light snow dusted the landscape, creating a serene yet stark contrast against the darkness. Grateful for his warm blanket and crackling fire, Salvatore sustained himself on his stash of dried figs and fresh water from the streams shimmering in the moonlight. The creeks flowed abundantly, their gentle sounds mingling with the rustle of leaves. Drawing upon his father's teachings, he set traps for small game. With the hunt of a few nimble rabbits and the occasional fish he skillfully caught, survival was within reach. Throughout his trek, Salvatore encountered only a handful of fellow travelers. Their exchanges were brief—a nod here, a pleasantry there—but he preferred to keep to himself, cloaked in the anonymity of his new name. As night enveloped the land, he pressed forward, a solitary figure against the vast canvas of an untamed wilderness, each step bringing him closer to a new beginning.

Salvatore managed to average about 15 kilometers per day. At this rate, he estimated that he would reach his new home in approximately 30 to 40 days, which would take him into November. If the nights in October were cool, he knew that November's nights would be a real challenge.

On November 13th, Salvatore finally saw something that lifted his spirits: a primitive sign indicating that Foiano di Val Fortore was just four kilometers away. He stopped to consider that by a strange stroke of fate, *he might enter the town on his birthday*. A certainty that he would never forget the date of the beginning of this new chapter of his life. He was weary from his travels and had not had a proper bath or shave since leaving Reggio di Calabria weeks earlier. The main road leading into the village of Foiano di Val Fortore was called "Strada Provinciale," which directed him straight to the town. The area was thickly forested, and Salvatore found it difficult to navigate through certain parts of the final leg of his journey. However, he realized that this was a good thing. His decision to relocate here was wise, as the town appeared even more remote than he had imagined. At this point, the simple map he had been using had lost its value, so he burned it in what would likely be the final campfire of his trip. His last campsite was about one kilometer from his destination. He decided to stop and sleep on a rocky outcrop that overlooked his future home. It was dark, perhaps around nine p.m., and he could barely make out some lights below. He would have to wait for dawn to see Foiano for the first time.

Chapter 8:
Introduction to Foiano di Val Fortore

Salvatore slept restlessly and awoke to a crisp autumn morning. A light dusting of snow had fallen overnight. The date was November 14, 1893. His campfire was still smoldering, and his stomach growled; he had not eaten a decent meal for more than two days. He mounted his horse and descended the steep slope toward the town of Foiano di Val Fortore. As he approached, he could see the commune laid out with low-slung stone and clay structures, most of which were one- or two-story buildings topped with red tile roofs. The tallest structure was a church steeple, perhaps ten meters high. As he entered the town proper, he began to see signs of life. The townsfolk were starting their day, whatever that might entail. Salvatore could tell that the town was likely settled in medieval times. The roads were primarily made of stones, and the uneven terrain made it difficult for his horse to walk except at a slow pace. As the newest visitor to this tiny village entered the town square, the citizens of Foiano di Val Fortore got their first look at Salvatore Teggiano. Concetta Maria Fisco was washing her family's clothes at the fountain when she saw the stranger for the first time. He sat stiffly atop the chestnut gelding, his head bobbing slightly as he turned slowly from left to right. He appeared tall, with very dark, almost black, wavy hair. His beard was thick and unkempt, and his clothes were shabby. It was unusual to see a stranger, especially at this time of year. Generally, the "operaios," or seasonal field workers, would appear in the spring or earlier during the harvest season. They would come to work the fertile fields surrounding Foiano and then disappear as agricultural needs dictated. Otherwise, strangers were indeed a rarity in her hometown.

The Fisco family proudly traced their lineage back several centuries to the very origins of Foiano. The locals affectionately referred to their village simply as "Foiano," while its residents were known as the Foianese. However, another town known as Foiano della Chiana exists in eastern Tuscany, nestled within the Arezzo region. This lesser-known Foiano was primarily an agricultural village, resting at the base of a picturesque valley near the winding Fortore River, bordered by majestic, towering mountains. Its landscape was characterized by rolling hills and patchwork fields, yet the town itself bore a striking resemblance to the myriad of other small communes scattered across this portion of Italy—isolated, modestly affluent, and home to a close-knit community where several dozen families had lived for generations. Families such as the Fiscos, Barbatos, Calabrese, Caruso, D'Andrea, Pacelli, Mercurio, Nardones, Romanos, Palumbo, and Zollos, among others, could trace their roots back over a thousand years, weaving a rich tapestry of history into the fabric of this humble village. On this day, as the sun began to rise from behind the mountains, casting a golden hue across the valley, a tall, enigmatic stranger rode into town, his purpose unknown. Unbeknownst to him, the quaint village was bustling with excitement as preparations unfolded for the annual celebration honoring its patron saint, San Giovanni Eremita, or Saint John the Hermit, a cherished event taking place every November 14th. Vibrant banners danced in the crisp November breeze, fluttering from wooden posts and charming balconies adorned with flowers. Salvatore observed the scene, sensing an air of anticipation and festivity. Women adorned in colorful skirts worked diligently to sweep the cobblestone walkways, and men perched high on ladders meticulously placed the finishing touches on the enchanting decorations that transformed the plaza. What was usually an unadorned gathering place was now a lively spectacle filled with cheerful signs, brightly colored banners, and fragrant floral arrangements. One prominent sign hanging from the grand façade of the large church on the east side of the square boldly proclaimed, "San Giovanni, proteggici sempre," meaning "Saint John, protect us always." Amidst this flurry of activity was Concetta Maria Fisco, a spirited sixteen-year-old girl with cascading long dark hair, expressive light brown eyes, and a slender figure. She was busy gathering her freshly washed clothes, carefully placing them into a wicker basket after wringing them out to remove excess water. As she hefted the now heavy basket, the tall stranger approached her, cloaked in an air of mystery. "Excuse me, miss, but could you point me to a place where I might rent a room?" he inquired, his voice smooth yet tinged with a hint of exhaustion. Concetta Maria paused; her gaze locked onto the handsome stranger for an extended moment. He bore the unmistakable scent of campfire smoke and slightly soiled linen, evoking a sense of rugged adventure that did little to impress her. With a tilt of her head, she gestured toward the large, inviting structure on the eastern side of the plaza—the church of the Most Holy Rosary—its steeple reaching gracefully toward the sky. "The church?" Salvatore asked, his brow furrowing in curiosity.

"Yes", said Concetta. "Talk to Father Ianotta. He can help you".

With that, the girl turned quickly and walked briskly away from the plaza.

Salvatore dismounted his horse and tied it to the weathered hitching post in front of the old stone church. He felt the fatigue of his long journey weigh heavily on his shoulders. With a resigned sigh, he made his way toward the modest rectory that flanked the ancient building, its crumbling facade a testament to years of weathering storms both literal and metaphorical. He raised a hand and knocked twice on the wooden door, the sound echoing in the stillness of the early morning. After a brief pause, the door creaked open to reveal a middle-aged woman. She had sharp features and dark hair pulled back into a tight bun, her eyes narrowing with a hint of skepticism as they assessed the stranger standing before her. "Si? Cosa vuoi?" she inquired, her voice tinged with curiosity yet laced with caution. Salvatore cleared his throat, conjuring what little energy he had left. "I am a weary traveler," he stated, his tone earnest. "I seek accommodations, a warm bath, and a meal. I assure you, I have money..." Before he could finish, a deep voice resonated from within. It belonged to a man who had likely been observing the exchange from his office behind the rectory door. "What's happening, Giovanna?" he called as he stepped into view. The priest approached with an air of cordiality, extending his right hand with a welcoming smile. Salvatore felt a flicker of relief; finally, someone here seemed friendly. "I am Father Mario Ianotta," he introduced himself with warmth. "My name is Teggiano. Salvatore Teggiano," Salvatore replied, the unfamiliarity of his new surname striking him momentarily. He couldn't shake the feeling that it marked a transformation in his identity, whether he welcomed it or not. "Ah, Sr. Teggiano," the priest exclaimed, his eyes brightening. "How delightful! Your name is the same as a village to the south of our town. Might you hail from there?" "Er, no," Salvatore stumbled slightly but quickly adapted to the thread of conversation. "I am, however, from the south," he added cautiously. "From where, may I ask?" Father Ianotta inquired, curiosity etched across his face. "From Scalia. It's a quaint fishing town by the coast..." Salvatore began, but before he could fully weave his tale,

Father Ianotta interjected with familiarity. "Indeed, Scalia... a fishing harbor, if I'm not mistaken. A charming little town renowned for its beautiful coastal views and rich waters, is it not?" Salvatore recognized the challenge ahead. He needed to tread carefully. "Yes, it is a small fishing town," he confirmed, with a hint of a defensive edge. "But I fear it's too small for a young man to make a living," he added, hoping to assuage any suspicions the priest might harbor. A thoughtful expression crossed Father Ianotta's face. "I see. And are you seeking your fortune here in the Fortore Valley?" he asked, genuinely intrigued.

"Well, not necessarily here in your town, Father, but perhaps somewhere along the way as I journey northward," he explained. Salvatore felt cautious about committing to a town filled with such inquisitive and suspicious people. The priest studied Salvatore, noting the condition of his clothing and his unkempt appearance. He also detected something peculiar about him—namely, his accent. Cocking his head to the side, he asked, "Sei Siciliano?" *The damned accent.* Salvatore thought quickly as he responded. "Very perceptive of you, Father. Yes, I was raised by relatives near Siracusa after my parents died. So, you see, some things are ingrained in us from an early age. However, I have spent most of my life in Italy." He wondered if that explanation was believable. The priest seemed satisfied. "Ah, I thought so. You see, I have an ear for accents, son," he said proudly, pointing to his ear. "Also, while studying for the priesthood in Rome, I met young men from far and wide, including Sicily, so I have been exposed to many dialects. I hope you don't think I am prying..." he added. "No, sir, not at all." "You are tired and need to eat and sleep before continuing on your long journey," he said. He directed his housekeeper to prepare a bed for his guest and to draw a bath. "You will have a hearty meal, and you will be my guest at the feast."

The priest was undoubtedly referring to the Feast of St. John. There was to be a procession, followed by a dinner and a Mass. Salvatore's first day in Foiano would be memorable.

Chapter 9:

Changes

———◆○◆———

While Salvatore luxuriated in the first bath he had taken in over a month, Giovanna, the housekeeper, washed his clothes and even took the time to mend them. When he toweled off, he found freshly laundered but still damp garments folded neatly at the foot of the single bed. He held them up to his nose and found they smelled new! Also on the bed were additional clothes: two flannel shirts, some undergarments, a pair of shoes, and a pair of neatly pressed trousers. He also discovered a pair of scissors, a hairbrush, and a straight razor. Salvatore carefully cut and then shaved off thirty days' worth of beard. He also trimmed his hair as much as he dared, combing it back. Father Ianotta provided him with some witch hazel, which Salvatore applied liberally to his newly shorn face. It stung, but ultimately, it felt good. He glanced at his pocket watch; it was twenty minutes to noon. Salvatore walked toward the kitchen, where Father Ianotta was seated at a large wooden table, facing away from him. Salvatore guessed that the priest was about fifty years old; he was tall, thin, and wore wire-rimmed eyeglasses. When Salvatore met him, the priest was dressed in a black cassock. Upon hearing Salvatore enter the room, Father Ianotta stood and turned to face him, now wearing an amice, an alb fastened with a cincture, and a richly decorated chasuble, the poncho-like vestment. Salvatore, not necessarily a devout Catholic, was nonetheless impressed by the priest's garments and could tell that the feast day of St. John was a major event in this town. "There you are," the priest said. "And look at you! You look, as they say, like a new man!" He smiled approvingly. "Thank you, Father," Salvatore replied. The priest was handed his zucchetto and his biretta, two pieces of headgear that completed his look for this important day. Salvatore thanked the housekeeper. Father Ianotta then spoke to Salvatore. "Now, my new friend, you will join us for the festivities. You are very fortunate to have come to our town on such an important day. You will join the procession, celebrate the Mass with us, and of course, eat like you have not eaten in a long time." The priest would not be dissuaded. Salvatore thanked him and followed the priest and his housekeeper out the door.

By noon in Foiano, the light coating of snow had melted under the midday sun, and the square was bustling with townsfolk. Salvatore estimated that nearly five hundred people had gathered near the church. The crowd murmured in respectful anticipation of the festivities. In the distance, he heard drums and coronets. Approaching the church was a band of about twelve musicians playing their instruments. Following closely behind them was a platform held at shoulder height by eight men. The wooden platform appeared heavy, measuring around eight feet long and four feet wide. It was adorned with bouquets of freshly cut flowers. Most impressive was the statue of San Giovanni Eremita, which swayed back and forth as the men carried it along the cobblestone road. Salvatore glanced to his right at the Church of the Most Holy Rosary. Standing on the steps near the top was Father Ianotta, who smiled serenely with his hands clasped at his chest. Women were beating their breasts, dressed in their finest dresses with their heads covered in silken cloth. The men, similarly attired in suit jackets, reverently held their caps over their hearts. Salvatore suddenly felt like someone was watching him. Why did he feel that way? No one knew him in this isolated town in Campania. However, Salvatore's instincts were correct. He quickly turned to his left and found the girl he had met when he rode into town. They had not been introduced, but it was Concetta Maria Fisco. She averted her eyes immediately as soon as she saw Salvatore looking directly at her. He noticed a beautiful young woman with big brown eyes and long hair tied back with a red ribbon, dressed simply but standing out among the crowd. A friend of hers, perhaps, stood nearby, and they giggled together as girls do. Concetta had likely told her friends about the scruffy yet handsome stranger she had unexpectedly encountered. Now, Concetta was intrigued by Salvatore, especially after he had bathed, shaved, and dressed respectably. For his part, Salvatore found himself smitten by the beautiful brunette, though he wasn't interested in pursuing a relationship; that was the farthest thing from his mind. November 14th marked the first time Salvatore had entered a church in many years. He took a seat near the back. The men reverently carried the statue of the anguished-looking patron saint toward the front and placed it on a pedestal. The church filled up with people, and those who could not find space inside stood on the steps and in the plaza. The front doors of the church were left open so everyone could hear and participate. Despite being a cynic about religion, Salvatore was impressed by the pomp and circumstance. The Mass lasted an hour, and Father Ionetta's homily was concise, even alluding to Salvatore anonymously. According to the priest, the good people of Foiano di Val Fortore should strive to "reach out to the poor, the weary, and the visitors." Again, Salvatore felt as if he was being observed.

Sure enough, across the aisle, Concetta was locking eyes with him. This time, an older gentleman stepped in, perhaps her father? As the Mass concluded, another elder stood beside the statue, inviting everyone to approach, to touch it, and to offer prayers for the sick and the departed. Father Ianotta took the opportunity to remind the congregation about the lavish dinner that awaited them. As Salvatore exited the church, he couldn't help but question the scarcity of women he had noticed inside. But as he stepped into the plaza, the reason became clear. Dozens of tables of all shapes and sizes—some long, others round—were arranged throughout the public square. The industrious women of the town had prepared both the food and the space for this grand celebration. The atmosphere transformed from solemnity to exuberance as it turned two p.m.; the townspeople of Foiano di Val Fortore would now revel in an afternoon of music, food, wine, and camaraderie. Before he could ponder his next move, a gentle grip on his elbow brought him back; it was the housekeeper. "Father asked me to introduce you to some of our wonderful citizens," she said, guiding him through the bustling crowd. "Will Father be joining us?" Salvatore inquired. "Absolutely. Come with me; you'll be sitting with him at the head table." The head table? Thus far, Salvatore had been attempting to blend in, but now, he was about to be presented to the entire town by its most esteemed leader. Reluctantly, Salvatore took his place of honor beside Father Mario Ianotta. Also at the table were the mayor, council members, and several influential businessmen with their wives. Surrounding them in the bustling square, hundreds of citizens raised their glasses in exuberant toasts to the patron saint, to the church, and to their cherished priest. These townsfolk certainly knew how to revel in joy. Salvatore realized that such occasions were likely rare, and his instincts proved right. Father Ianotta leaned in, his voice sincere. "This celebration marks the pinnacle of the lives of the people here in Foiano. Please don't mistake their joy for frivolity. They are sober, humble, and hard-working individuals. This feast day unites them in a way that is truly special." "I understand, Father. I just... I don't feel worthy to be at this table..." The cleric quickly interjected. "You must not harbor such thoughts, my son. We want you to feel at home here. After all, as it is written in Leviticus, 'When a foreigner resides among you in your land, do not mistreat them. The foreigner residing among you must be treated as your native-born. Love them as yourself, for you were foreigners in Egypt. I am the LORD your God.'" With this, Father Ianotta raised his glass of wine, clinking it against Salvatore's, inviting him into a moment that signified unity and warmth, a true embrace of hospitality.

"I want to introduce you to my family as well. I have two sisters who live here. We are all one great family!" Moments after the cleric's welcoming remarks and prayer, Father Ionotta offered a traditional toast and called upon the servers to bring out the delicacies for the hungry guests. Salvatore savored his first glass of wine in over a month and gladly accepted another. Every table was adorned with pitchers of deep red, dry wine. He noticed that most of the servers were women from the village, including some young girls. One of the servers, Concetta Maria Fisco, wore the same dress she had worn to church, now accompanied by a crisp white cotton apron to protect it. The feast featured delicacies one might expect from a mountain village situated far from the seacoast. Foianese specialties included lamb, mutton, pecorino, and goat's milk cheese, along with olive oil, wines, hot peppers, and saffron. Like most peasant cuisines, the food in the Fortore Valley was simple yet wholesome. Lamb and mutton were favored meats, but pork was also popular inland, with many families raising animals in a semi-wild state, allowing them to forage in the forests and butchering them in the fall. Olive oil played a significant role in the region's cooking, alongside cereals and grains grown in the limited flat areas. Some of that grain was transformed into pasta—especially the famous orecchiette, or ear-shaped pasta—and some was made into bread. Foiano was renowned for its bread, and throughout the region, one could find friselle, which are discs of dried bread rehydrated in water and topped with olive oil, capers, and fresh tomatoes. Salvatore considered himself fortunate to be in this region following the harvest, allowing him to indulge in the rich yet simple aromas, textures, and flavors of the feast. As for the people, their initially standoffish nature seemed to dissipate once they observed the passion with which Father Mario Ionotta welcomed their guest. Salvatore realized that above all others in the small community, Father Ionotta was the unchallenged leader. Concetta somehow took on the responsibility of attending to the needs of those seated at the head table. Salvatore noticed that initially, another young lady had that responsibility, but now it was Concetta. Father Ionotta seemed to recognize the attraction between Concetta and Salvatore. "Concetta is my sister's daughter," he noted proudly. "My sister's husband is the town barber, so I am certain he would be happy to provide you with a professional haircut. Consider it a treat, courtesy of me." Concetta overheard their conversation as she refilled the wine glasses. "My father is an excellent barber," she said. "But you shouldn't get your hair cut too short…" Realizing she might come off as too eager, Concetta caught herself and changed the subject. "Ahh, my dear niece has such a strong opinion about men's hairstyles," Father Ionotta joked. Concetta blushed, averted her eyes, and quickly left the table. "My niece is a very beautiful young woman, isn't she?" Salvatore contemplated. "She is indeed beautiful. May I ask, how old is she?" "Concetta recently turned sixteen. In Foiano, she is considered a woman," the cleric replied. This statement could be interpreted as an invitation for Salvatore to pursue Concetta romantically. While Salvatore was interested, he remained extremely cautious, unsure if it was wise to stay in Foiano. As the meal progressed, Father Ionotta shared the story of San Giovanni Eremita with a curious Salvatore. "The hermit Giovanni da Tufara was born, raised, and buried here in the Fortore Valley," the priest explained. "He was chosen by Pope Hadrian IV to found a monastery when he was wise enough at seventy years old. This occurred around 1156 A.D. San Giovanni is credited with instilling in the monastery a great desire to connect with this region and its people, aiming to free them from the backwardness of that era. He elevated our people's spirit and is remembered and revered for redeeming their dignity to this day," Father Ionotta said. Before San Giovanni's arrival, the Fortore Valley was considered very primitive and desolate. The monastery brought civilization, empowering the various communities with organized governance and codified laws.

Salvatore stood amidst the vibrant festivities of Foiano di Val Fortore, where the air was alive with the sounds of laughter, music, and the tantalizing aroma of traditional dishes being prepared. He couldn't help but witness the reverence in the eyes of the townspeople as they celebrated their beloved patron saint, San Giovanni. For centuries, the descendants of this quaint village had paid homage to the man who had skillfully orchestrated peace among the warring Byzantines, Longobards, and Normans. Curiosity bubbling within him, Salvatore turned to the elderly priest beside him, his voice a mix of intrigue and wonder. "Father, what is the significance of holding the feast on this date, November 14th?" The priest smiled warmly, his face etched with the wisdom of many harvests. "November 14th, my son, is the day that San Giovanni passed away," he replied, his voice reverberating with deep respect and a hint of solemnity.

Under ordinary circumstances, this kind of information would have elicited little more than a dismissive shrug from an agnostic like Salvatore. Raised in an atmosphere where the only doctrines preached were those of power and influence, thanks to his father's unwavering belief in money and power, the religious significance would have gone largely unnoticed. Yet today, something was different. Perhaps it was the enchanting ambiance of the festival, with its colorful decorations and animated celebrations, or the delightful array of local wines he had indulged in, each sip igniting a warmth that spread through him. As he experienced this unexpected levity, Salvatore found himself captivated by the tales spun around him. For the first time in months, he began to entertain the notion that this isolated village might not just be a passing phase but a place where he could truly settle down, cultivate connections, and perhaps even plant the roots he had long evaded. However, this new aspiration weighed heavily on his mind. To embrace this fresh chapter, Salvatore would need to relinquish his past, leaving behind a career and life he had once fiercely known. The thought sent a ripple of uncertainty through him, even as the joy of the festival swirled around him.

Chapter 10:
A Turn of Events

The feast continued until dark, around five o'clock in the evening. The mid-November air began to chill, and people started cleaning up after the daylong celebration. Salvatore assisted in the cleanup and found himself feeling refreshed by the socialization, making new acquaintances in the small town. He might have been introduced to ninety percent of the residents of Foiano di Val Fortore. Men shook his hand, and both men and women greeted him with kisses on each cheek, as was the town's custom. Very quickly, Salvatore Teggiano felt that he had become part of Foiano. In this still isolated valley, gaining acceptance from the community was highly unusual. The town had been predominantly occupied by the same families for centuries. The name Teggiano was unknown to the Foianese, but the usual suspicions were alleviated by Father Ionotta's immediate embrace of the stranger. It seemed that the priest's approval was enough for the one thousand people who comprised the community. Even Father Ionotta chipped in, helping the men move the heavy wooden tables and benches from the square. As Salvatore joined in, he overheard some men discussing him. "Will he stay?" one man asked another. "If he does, what kind of work will he find?" Salvatore began to wonder about this himself.

The answers to where he would stay and what he would do would come very soon. Once again, Father Ionotta would provide the answers.

As cleanup progressed and neared its end, Giovanna, the housekeeper, called to Salvatore. "Father wants to talk to you at the rectory," she said, pointing toward the church. Salvatore finished what he was doing and then walked dutifully across the square to the priest's residence. There, he found Father Ionotta waiting for him. "I have some news for you, my new friend." Salvatore felt somewhat unsettled by the trust and friendship he was being shown. He was a man on the run, with blood on his hands. He had been dishonest even regarding his identity, which began to fill him with guilt. "We have found a place for you to live," the priest said. Not just a place to stay but "a place to reside." This was surprising. Before Salvatore could respond, the priest continued. "And in addition, I have found you a job. Not just any job, but I dare say a trade. My brother-in-law has agreed to take you on as an apprentice in the barber trade." Salvatore was at a loss for words. The barber trade? This was something he had never considered. A lowly barber, a man who cuts hair and shaves the faces of strangers for hardly any money. "This cannot be happening," he thought to himself. His expression must have given him away, for the priest noticed the look of disappointment on Salvatore's face. Salvatore felt ashamed; this man was going out of his way to help him. Then, he suddenly brightened and smiled broadly. "I am... unworthy of your kindness, Father," he said. "Nonsense. You are a guest, and you are in need. It is the least we can do. You told me that you had no home and were searching for an opportunity," the priest replied.

The older gentleman was indeed correct; this was precisely what Salvatore had communicated to him only hours prior. Within a remarkably short period, the man had made considerable efforts to welcome Salvatore, ensuring he felt integrated into a larger family unit. He had provided food, clothing, and now, a place to live, in addition to assistance in securing a livelihood. Salvatore ought to regard this unexpected turn of good fortune with some appreciation, particularly given the string of misfortunes he had endured over the preceding weeks. "I accept your offer, Father. I shall endeavor to learn the trade," Salvatore responded. He quickly perceived that establishing roots and engaging in a profession would enhance his relatively brief stay in this town. "Excellent. Now, please accompany me to my sister's residence; it is not far from here," the priest instructed. As Salvatore followed Father Ionotta, with his satchel in hand, his thoughts raced. The Fisco family would be his hosts. Signore Fisco would take him on as an apprentice, and Concetta Maria Fisco, their attractive young daughter, would also be present. Upon reaching the door, Mrs. Fisco answered Father Ionotta's light knock. "Antoinette, as promised, here is the young man," she announced. If the priest's sister harbored any surprise regarding the arrangement, she concealed it skillfully. She extended her hands to grasp Salvatore's with warmth. "Welcome. Please, come inside," she invited with sincerity. She then guided Salvatore and Father Ionotta to the modest parlor. "Please, take a seat," she instructed. Shortly thereafter, she called for the remainder of the family to join them. Within moments, Signore Fisco, their fourteen-year-old son Anthony, and eventually Concetta entered. Concetta had changed into a different dress, and her hair was unbound, enhancing her radiant appearance. "Here you are. As promised, Salvatore, you shall remain with my family," Father Ionotta declared. Salvatore's gaze traversed from one face to another, seeking any indication that this arrangement was against someone's wishes. As a stranger in this setting, he contemplated that none were aware of his background or intentions; for all they knew, he might have been a bandit or, as was the reality, a fugitive from justice. All eyes remained focused on him, conveying nothing but genuine pleasure about the arrangement. The nervous silence in the small room was shattered by an unexpected, loud coughing fit from Signore Fisco, accompanied by a peculiar gurgling sound unfamiliar to Salvatore. "We wish for you to feel at home, young man," stated Signora Fisco. Concetta's father added, "Our home is your home for as long as you desire to stay." Their expressions were wholly sincere. The young boy, prompted by his father, extended his hand to shake Salvatore's. Subsequently, Concetta Maria stepped forward. Salvatore found himself momentarily transfixed. She was petite, with fair skin and striking light brown eyes that appeared to gaze deep into his soul. For the first time, she was looking directly at him. She offered her right hand, and he accepted it with both of his, feeling a sudden surge of emotion as his heart began to race. Her hand was soft, and he could not divert his gaze from her. Concetta stood approximately five feet six inches tall, a height greater than that of many women. Her father was nearly as tall as Salvatore, suggesting the source of her stature. As his thoughts swirled, he inhaled the delicate fragrance of her hair. Concetta spoke, but he did not register her words.

"I hope that you will be happy here," she repeated. He was a man of twenty-three, and here, he was captivated by a sixteen-year-old. "Y-yes, I'm certain that I will be happy here." He looked around nervously, trying to gauge if his uncertainty was evident to everyone. Anthony was giggling. Mrs. Fisco nodded approvingly, but Sr. Fisco's expression remained stern and unchanged. "Good, good," the priest continued. "I will see to it that your horse is brought here to you," he promised. He turned halfway toward the front door as he added, "Ciao." Before he knew it, Concetta had disappeared. Mrs. Fisco was showing him to the room he would share with Anthony. Sr. Fisco asked Salvatore to put his belongings away and then join him in the parlor for a discussion. Salvatore complied. Soon, he found himself with the older man. Sr. Fisco was tall, thin, and somewhat taciturn. Generally, a man of few words, he was well-respected in Foiano. In addition to being the town barber, Michele Fisco also served as the town's surgeon. It was a common practice among small-town barbers to double as medical providers when the need arose. Just earlier that week, Michele Fisco had removed a growth from the arm of a neighbor. He was also a member of the town council, so it was clear to Salvatore that this was one of the more respected and prominent families in the valley. Mrs. Fisco had prepared two small glasses of Anisette. As Sr. Fisco sipped his, Salvatore nervously swallowed his in a single gulp. Mrs. Fisco poured another drink, left the bottle, and disappeared. "Salvatore," Fisco said, clearing his throat, "I hold great respect for my brother-in-law, Father Ionotta." Salvatore's mind raced. "Because of this deep respect, I have agreed to offer you a place to stay and to teach you my trade." The older man got up, walked to the window, and glanced outside at the now darkened landscape. He returned to his chair and offered Salvatore another glass of the liqueur. Salvatore accepted. "I feel you should know that we are not in the habit of opening our home to strangers, to those we do not know," he said. Salvatore responded, "Believe me, Sr. Fisco, this was more my father's idea than mine. I can understand your hesitance, and for that reason, I will leave right now if you and your family are in any way uncomfortable." Salvatore spoke with great sincerity. The older man looked closely at his face as he spoke. "No, you are our guest, and as Father stated, you are welcome here. I expect you to join me in my shop for breakfast tomorrow. There is much to learn."

The job interview had come to a close, yet Salvatore sensed that Sr. Fisco's gaze held deeper intentions that first night. Had the father detected something in the way Salvatore locked eyes with his daughter or in the unspoken chemistry that flickered between him and Concetta? With a growing awareness, Salvatore understood he needed to tread carefully when it came to his interactions with her father. As dawn barely kissed the horizon on November 15th, a sudden rattle jolted Salvatore from his peaceful sleep. His new roommate, Anthony Fisco, seemed to take immense delight in waking him as if it were a game. Through the thin walls, he could hear the unsettling sound of Mr. Fisco coughing, a raspy reminder of the morning. "Svegliati! Mamma ha preparato la colazione per te e devi andare a lavorare!" (Wake up! Mom has prepared breakfast for you, and you need to go to work!) With a shiver, Salvatore's bare feet met the cold, wooden floor, instantly awakening his senses. He splashed water on his face and dressed quickly, inhaling the rich, inviting aroma of freshly brewed café latte wafting in from the kitchen. As he stepped into the warmth of the dining room, he found Mr. and Mrs. Fisco along with Anthony, already gathered around the family table, their voices mingling in morning chatter. But where was Concetta? The absence of her presence added a layer of intrigue to the otherwise busy scene.

He took his place at the table as Mrs. Fisco poured a cup of café latte. Anthony was drinking hot milk, and Sr. Fisco sipped his coffee while eating yogurt. "What can I make for you?" she asked. "We have some fresh yogurt, nice fette biscottate, or rolls with jam…" "Biscottate, please," he replied. Mrs. Fisco quickly served him the cookie-like hard bread. Salvatore noticed that in this part of Italy, breakfasts were like those in his former home in southern Sicily: spare and simple. Sr. Fisco inquired whether Salvatore had slept well. "Well enough, thank you," he answered. "Are you prepared to learn a new trade today?" asked Sr. Fisco. "Yes, sir. I am very much looking forward to learning…" he lied. Once breakfast was finished, the two men left the house and walked a few hundred yards down the steep hill from the Fisco home. Soon, they arrived at the town square. Catty-corner from the church was a small white stucco building with a wooden sign out front that read, "M. Fisco, Barbiere." Michele Fisco unlocked the wooden door, and Salvatore followed him inside. It was dawn, and the early morning sun of November was just beginning to rise. Michele lit a kerosene lamp, hung up his coat, and invited Salvatore to do the same. He placed a pan of water on top of the wood stove. Salvatore surveyed the room, which was about three-by-three meters.

There was a window next to the front door, a mirror along the wall, and a countertop containing the barbering tools: scissors, combs, shaving implements, and a strop. Two chairs lined the opposite wall, presumably for customers waiting their turn. In the center of the room was a chair for the person receiving the service. Sr. Fisco began to cough violently, bending at the waist. He held a white fazzoletto (handkerchief) over his nose and mouth. Salvatore noticed it had turned red with the older man's blood. "How much do you charge for a haircut? A shave?" Salvatore asked, trying to divert attention from what he had just witnessed. The older man stared at him for a long ten seconds. "Young man, you will soon learn that not everything in this world revolves around money." Michele began to sharpen his straight razor. "In a poor village like this, currency is in short supply. We tend to barter for services. For example, Signore Caruso has some of the best lemons in the valley, so we trade my services for a bushel of fine fruits." Salvatore nodded. "Signore Pacelli raises pigs. For two months of haircuts, I receive a small pig. Another farmer may trade corn or tomatoes… and that is how we do business here." He stared at the razor, licked his left thumb, and tested its sharpness. Perfect.

"Sit," he commanded with an air of authority. Salvatore, a young man with unkempt hair and worn features, complied and lowered himself into the chair positioned squarely in the center of the warmly lit room. Michele Fisco, the barber, draped a pristine white linen over him, the fabric stark against Salvatore's darker clothing. With deliberate movements, he approached the stove and retrieved a clean, white towel, which he plunged into the bubbling, steamy water. After wringing it out, he gently placed the warm towel on Salvatore's face, the heat soothing against his skin. As he worked, Michele spoke with a hint of pride in his voice. "You are about to receive your first civilized shave and haircut in quite a long time. I can tell, especially from the state of your hair." The comforting warmth enveloped Salvatore's face, and for a moment, he allowed himself to relax. Mr. Fisco lifted the towel and carefully lathered Salvatore's beard with a rich, frothy mixture. With a flourish, he produced a gleaming, menacing-looking straight razor, its blade reflecting the soft light of the room. With practiced skill, he began the meticulous process of shaving, each precise stroke removing the weeks of neglect from Salvatore's complexion. Before long, the job was done, and Salvatore, tentatively reaching beneath the linen, touched his newly smooth face. "Pretty good, no?" Michele asked, a sly grin spreading across his face. "Very good!" Salvatore replied enthusiastically, a spark of confidence returning to his demeanor. "Next, the hair. I was told by Concetta, not too short…" They both erupted into laughter, the sound filling the intimate space. Ten minutes later, Salvatore stood before a large, ornate mirror, his reflection revealing a transformed man. For the first time in what felt like an eternity, he looked well-groomed, his features highlighted in a way he had long forgotten. "Thank you, sir," he said, his voice brimming with gratitude. "I am prepared to pay you, not with eggs, lemons, or even a pig, but with actual currency," he stated firmly, eyeing Michele with a mixture of seriousness and levity. Michele's eyes widened in disbelief, momentarily overwhelmed by the shock of it all. He couldn't fathom how a person in Salvatore's situation could possess money. "I will pay you when we return to our home," Salvatore continued, suddenly anxious that he had made a slip. Surely, it would raise suspicion that a wandering soul like him had cash on hand. As Salvatore swept up the remnants of his grooming session, he heard the door creak open. Poking his head into the room was Giovanni Capuano, a middle-aged man exuding a warm familiarity. "Buongiorno. Sono troppo presto o posso farmi tagliare i capelli ora?" he inquired, his voice deep and robust. Michele's face lit up with a broad smile. Giovanni was not just a client; he was an old friend. The two men embraced heartily, the warmth of their friendship evident in their body language. Michele gestured for Giovanni to take a seat in the same chair that had just been occupied. "Salvatore... take my friend's coat, please," Michele instructed. Giovanni settled into the chair, and their jovial conversation flowed easily for a few moments. Giovanni Capuano, a burly figure at around five-foot-ten and tipping the scales at an easy 200 pounds, wore a rugged flannel shirt, heavy woolen trousers, and sturdy worker's shoes still crusted with dry mud from the fields. "Make me beautiful," he proclaimed with a chuckle, his smile infectious. "Giovanni, I would like you to meet a friend..." Michele began, but Giovanni interrupted with familiarity. "Yes, yes, I know all about the stranger. Salvatore is his name, hailing from the southern regions. Just passing through..." Salvatore silently mourned the lack of privacy in such a tight-knit village. News had evidently spread quickly about his stay with the Fiscos, leaving little room for secrets in this small community.

Giovanni leaned against the worn wooden counter, his arms crossed, and continued, "Welcome to the Fortore Valley. If I may inquire, how long do you plan to stay in this desolate place? Hardly anyone chooses to remain here, do they, Michele?" Before Michele had a chance to respond, Giovanni continued his lament. "There is virtually nothing here: sparse businesses, dwindling job opportunities, and an overwhelming sense of stagnation," he sighed dramatically. "As for myself, I'm saving every penny to escape this valley as soon as I can." Finally, Michele seized the moment to speak. "Giovanni, with all due respect, you've been planning to move away for as long as I've known you." Giovanni straightened up, a spark of determination in his eyes. "This time, I truly mean it," he insisted. Michele skillfully tied the sheet around the man's neck in reparation of his work. Giovanni continued. "Michele, you know I speak the truth. I, for one, labor tirelessly on land that will never truly belong to me, all for the benefit of some distant landlord, twenty kilometers away. He pays me a scant wage for the toil of tilling, planting, nurturing, and harvesting crops, while he takes all the profits for himself." Michele attempted to inject some optimism into the conversation. "But you manage to live well, don't you? You've survived." Giovanni, unable to mask his frustration, stood up sharply. He yanked the sheet from around his neck and dramatically flung it over a nearby chair. "Rubbish! No man should be forced to grovel for survival. I will forge my destiny and create my fortune far away from here." With that proclamation, he donned his coat and stormed out, leaving a trail of scattered energy behind him. Michele stood there, momentarily taken aback, then shrugged nonchalantly, shaking out the sheet as a reflex and starting to fold it expertly. "He'll return; he always does," he remarked with a knowing smile. After a brief silence, Salvatore broke in with curiosity, "What did he mean by making a fortune somewhere far away?" Michele chuckled, his eyes twinkling with amusement. "Ah, Giovanni is nothing if not a dreamer. He has been spinning tales for years. There was this one person from our town who left a few years back and settled in America. He regularly sends back letters and postcards to his relatives in Foiano, gushing about how magnificent life is over there. He claims the streets are paved with gold and that they hand you a pick and shovel to dig for riches." Michele shook his head with a laugh as he carefully placed the freshly cleaned linen on the table. "So, you don't buy his tales of America, then?" Salvatore asked, a skeptical brow raised. Michele's expression grew serious as he replied, "Salvatore, I'm sure of very few things in this world, but one thing is certain: a man is defined by his own character, and that is something that cannot be changed by dreams or distant lands." And with that profound thought hanging in the air, Salvatore's eagerly awaited first lesson in hair cutting would have to be postponed a little longer.

Chapter 11:

Eighteen Ninety-Four

As November transitioned into December, the new year of 1894 was approaching for Salvatore Treggiano and his adopted home of Foiano di Val Fortore. Since his arrival, Salvatore had been welcomed into the community, found a home, learned a trade, and begun courting Concetta Maria Fisco. Concetta would turn seventeen in December, while Salvatore had turned twenty-four. In Italy, neither age was considered too young for marriage and starting a family. From Salvatore's viewpoint, it seemed that everyone who mattered was in favor of him and the daughter of Mr. and Mrs. Fisco becoming engaged. Father Ionotta often spoke glowingly about his niece to Salvatore, and when they were alone, he frequently praised the young man's looks, habits, and manners to his niece. Even the Fisco family seemed to warm up to the idea of this match. In this part of Italy, matchmaking was commonplace. Most young women found themselves paired with someone's nephew or son. Many of these connections were likely to end in disappointment or failure, as people with mismatched personalities were often thrown together. However, in the case of Concetta and Salvatore, there was genuine physical attraction. Whenever Concetta saw Salvatore, she found herself examining every inch of him and imagining physical contact with him. Being a devoutly religious young lady, Concetta often confessed her impure thoughts to her uncle almost every week. At first, Uncle Mario dismissed it as typical teenage behavior, but soon he connected her thoughts to the new arrival in town. He smiled to himself, acted sternly, and prescribed five Hail Marys and five Our Fathers as penance, along with a directive to "refrain from future impure thoughts and deeds!" On his part, Salvatore had started attending Mass every Sunday with the Fisco family, a significant change from his former life. He discovered that the Fiscos were very devout Catholics. Concetta was receiving an education alongside several other girls from Foiano at a convent a few kilometers outside of town. Anthony attended classes at the local school. Most children, particularly girls like Concetta, typically completed their education by the age of twelve, and pursuing further education beyond sixth grade was uncommon. Father Ionotta considered Concetta to be "extremely bright," which earned her the privilege of extra schooling. In the rural villages of Campania, education beyond elementary school was rare, as children were expected to help their parents scrape by in a mostly agricultural lifestyle. Many families worked as sharecroppers, tending to the lands owned by a few wealthy landowners. In some extreme cases, parents "loaned out" their children as workers, some as young as ten or twelve years old. Concetta's family relied on her father's trade, which, during prosperous times, generated monetary income. More often, however, Michele Fisco kept his family afloat by bartering goods and services, as he explained to Salvatore. For Salvatore, this existence was something he dreaded. Coming from a poor background in a rural area of Sicily, he found this life particularly unsettling. Unlike the peasants around him, Salvatore Arcuri's father would never accept his lot in life. Francesco "Il Leone" was a proud man who dared to be independent from "i ricchi proprietari terrier," or the wealthy landowners.

As the family gathered around the dinner table, savoring homemade pasta and fragrant tomato sauce, Salvatore's thoughts drifted to the angry figure he had encountered earlier at the barbershop—Giovanni Capuano. Giovanni was a man consumed by frustration and desperation, preparing to leave the picturesque valley of Foiano to seek what he called a "new life" in America. Salvatore felt a growing understanding of the unspoken sadness that hung over many in their tight-knit community, a shared sense of longing for something more. After the last bite of dinner had been swallowed and the dishes cleared away, Sr. Fisco stepped outside into the cool evening air, lighting his pipe with a practiced hand. The comforting scent of tobacco wafted through the dimming light as Concetta, having finished her chores, joined her father on the porch. Salvatore could hear fragments of their conversation, the folds of their words tinged with worry. Concetta spoke in hushed tones, recounting a troubling situation with a man who supervised the field workers, explaining how he had been abusive towards her. Her voice trembled as she recalled the latest incident, and Salvatore's heart ached for her as he listened. Michele, her father, wore a pained expression while absorbing her sobbing confession, but he seemed at a loss for how to protect her. Unfortunately, the reality was stark: there were no authorities to whom they could turn for help. In the end, he simply urged her to "be strong," his words filled with a father's love yet laced with helplessness. Later that night, as the house settled into silence, Salvatore ambled past the closed door of Concetta's room. He could hear her quiet sobs seeping through the wood, a haunting sound that pierced through the stillness. Softly, he knocked on her door. "Yes?" she asked, her voice quivering with uncertainty. "It's me, Salvatore. Can we talk?" he replied gently. "Talk about what?" Concetta responded, her tone defensive as she refused to open the door. Understanding the walls she had built around herself, Salvatore sighed and retreated to his own room, unable to shake the worry for his friend. By February, after months of dedicated practice in the barbering trade, Salvatore had become quite adept at cutting hair and performing shaves. He recalled the early days where shaky hands had led to a few close calls with the razor, but now he felt a growing confidence in his skills. He was capable enough to run the shop in Michele's absence, which had become more frequent as the older man started spending time in the fields. Despite Sr. Fisco's declining health, he now trusted Salvatore enough to take over the barbering responsibilities. Yet, as the days turned into weeks, Salvatore's concern for Concetta deepened. He often observed her distressed demeanor on the days she would head to the farm, where the shadows of her troubles seemed to linger. Nothing had changed, and the weight of her burden hung heavily in the air. Caught in his thoughts, Salvatore couldn't help but compare the timid barber with the fierce protector he envisioned in his own father, Ill Leone. If his father were in this situation, he would have confronted the man responsible for harming Concetta without hesitation. Now, Salvatore found himself torn, struggling with the choice between remaining anonymous and risking everything to stand up for Concetta against the man who had caused her so much pain.

As winter turned to spring, suddenly, Concetta's attitude toward Salvatore changed. She paid more attention to him, and they were soon taking long walks around the village. On April 29th, Concetta reached down to hold his hand. She did not look at him, but the touch of her hand in his made him take notice. It was as though she suddenly was sending a message to him. Salvatore stopped and turned toward her. "Concetta, I, I..." Before he could finish, she put both of her hands upon his face. She drew him close and offered her lips to him. Salvatore's heart began to pound. Although he had been with many women, *none had been pure*. They were women of questionable morals, and he never felt any feeling other than ultimate contempt for them and their easy ways.

Concetta whispered softly. "I am in love with you", she said. "I don't have any idea why, but I am in love with you".

Salvatore savored the moment. He collected himself. He spoke. "Concetta, from the first moment that we met, I also had feelings for you".

"Do you mean there in the town square, when you were dirty and smelly, on the horse?" she asked. She was smiling, then a hearty laugh. "I can't say that I was in love at that beginning", she said. He smiled.

"Then when?" he asked.

Concetta looked down, then straight into his eyes. "The night that you came to my door and wanted to talk with me. You were interested in me, in why I was sad", she said. Tears formed in her eyes as she recounted the incident.

Salvatore wiped away the tears and kissed her again.

"No one has ever cared for me before." she started to walk away. "When I am with you, I feel that, that you care about me", she continued. "Do you?"

"Do I what...?"

"Care for me?" The answer came quickly, naturally. "Concetta, I love you very much and I want you."

Chapter 12:
Concetta Maria

In May of 1894, several significant events took place. First, Salvatore approached the Fiscos to ask for their daughter's hand in marriage. Later, he engaged in a series of interesting discussions with Giovanni Capuano. The two men developed a friendship, often meeting at the shop, regardless of whether Giovanni needed service, to discuss various topics such as the day's events, the weather, the lemon crops, or the state of the economy in Fortore. The latter topic seemed to excite Capuano the most. "I am closer than anyone thinks to making my move," he said one day. "Do you remember me talking about Carlo Zollo?" "Zollo?" Salvatore replied, pondering. "Ah yes, he's the fellow you worked with—your cousin, I believe." Salvatore felt proud that he remembered this detail. "Yes, my cousin. Well, you haven't seen him in many months, have you?" Salvatore had only met Carlo Zollo once, but he played along. "What became of him?" he asked. Giovanni became animated. "He went to America! He traveled to Napoli, got on a ship, and sailed off." He pointed west. "America, I presume," said Salvatore. "Yes, and I am next. Carlo's brother left earlier. They are working there, and he is planning to send for me. All one needs is a sponsor. The sponsor arranges a job, a place to live, and of course, must vouch for my character." "Well, you certainly are a character," Salvatore joked, and both men shared a good laugh. Giovanni continued, "Salvatore, I know that you feel trapped living here. You can't possibly be happy in this place. I can bring you to America..." Salvatore interrupted. "Wait a minute. You haven't left yet, and you're already inviting me along? Talk sense, Giovanni," he said. "Besides, I will soon be married, then children..." Giovanni quickly interjected, "And into this world, you want to bring a family?" This comment stopped Salvatore in his tracks. Giovanni was right. There was no future for him or his future wife and children in Foiano di Val Fortore. After all, Salvatore Arcuri was the son of "Ill Leone," and a man in his position needed above all to provide for his sons. This mere dot on a map could never fulfill his destiny. Perhaps surprisingly to most in Foiano, Giovanni Capuano said his goodbyes and made his way to Naples. There, he would board a ship and embark on a journey across the ocean towards an uncertain future. Salvatore would miss his lively friend and felt a mix of trepidation for both Giovanni and him, as they both faced an uncertain path ahead.

"I will write to you, and I promise that I will bring you over," he declared with unwavering confidence. Giovanni's hands clasped Salvatore's shoulders tightly, his grip firm and reassuring. "But now, my friend, you must promise me something," he continued, his voice low and earnest. Salvatore met Giovanni's gaze, a flicker of apprehension in his eyes. "When your time comes, you too shall join me there," Giovanni insisted. With a heavy heart, Salvatore nodded, assuring him he would consider this significant promise. As Giovanni prepared to depart for Naples, a sense of finality filled the air. Salvatore couldn't shake the ominous feeling that this might be the last time he ever heard from his dear friend. The courtship between Salvatore Teggiano and Concetta Marie Fisco had blossomed, nearing the culmination of a wedding to be blessed by her beloved uncle. The barbershop, once overseen by Michele Fisco, now lay squarely in Salvatore's hands as Michele's health deteriorated alarmingly. The winter of 1893-94 was cruel; Michele suffered from a relentless illness known as "The Consumption," rendering him bedridden for long, agonizing stretches. With each passing day, the weight of responsibility pressed heavily on Salvatore's shoulders, a burden he bore with solemn dignity. Two letters had arrived from Giovanni, the first one penned in the bustling atmosphere of New York City, postmarked from the iconic Ellis Island. Giovanni vividly recounted the horrors of his voyage—a turbulent journey rife with uncertainty—but there was hope. He had met Carlo, an old acquaintance who had promised to guide him through the bewildering process of entry into this strange new land. Then, two months later, another letter fluttered in, bearing the distinct postmark of "South Bethlehem Pennsylvania." The name alone sparked curiosity—where on God's green earth was Pennsylvania? In his vibrant narrative, Giovanni painted a picture of South Bethlehem, a city alive with industry and opportunity, where jobs lay waiting, even for those like him who spoke little English. With a thrumming heart, Salvatore imagined the scene: a cacophony of whirring machines, the furious clanging of factory bells, and the churning of wheels, surrounded by a melting pot of cultures—Slavs, Germans, and a growing community of fellow Italians. Giovanni shared tales of camaraderie amongst the Italians, each helping the other navigate the challenges of their new home. He had quickly secured a room in a boarding house, found a small loan, and above all, landed a paying job. Though it was only a janitorial position at the train station, Giovanni reveled in the fact that it granted him the luxurious sum of four US dollars a week—an amount that made him feel like a king. Giovanni Capuano's bold leap into the unknown resonated deeply with Salvatore, reminding him of his own courageous decision to leave Sicily behind. But the thought of embarking on a journey to America hammered at his heart with greater intensity. He now bore a family to consider, a wife and a future he needed to protect. Salvatore wrestled with the enormity of such a decision. This choice would ripple through the lives of Concetta's parents and her brother, all of whom had shown him kindness and support during his struggles. How could he bear to abandon them after all they had done for him? While the allure of economic opportunities in America tugged at his spirit, Salvatore knew he must tread carefully. He needed to prepare for this monumental shift, not just for himself, but for those tied to him by love and loyalty. Furthermore, he felt compelled to confront a pressing matter that gnawed at his conscience—the conduct of the farm foreman, Ettore Umberto, who had crossed a line with Concetta. While she had refrained from detailing the nature of his transgressions, Salvatore's heart seethed with righteous indignation. It was enough for him to know that this man had dared to tarnish the dignity of the woman he loved. Ettore Umberto's actions were intolerable, and Salvatore's code of honor demanded retribution. He could not allow such an affront to pass unchallenged. Determined and resolute, he steeled himself to face the man who had dared to take liberties with his innocent bride-to-be.

All through the month of May, Salvatore planned his revenge. Salvatore's father spoke sparingly about revenge to his son over the years. He was fond of saying that "A man who desires revenge should dig two graves." Salvatore grew to understand the meaning and noted that his father was more calculating than many other men in his world. He considered blood as an expense and unnecessary violence and bloodshed should be avoided and should be used only as a last resort. Salvatore learned this lesson the hard way when he went over the line and murdered Massimo Neri. That lack of self-control resulted in the death of his father and started a destructive war.

But if it was Salvatore Teggiano's intention to begin his life anew with a different identity, in a new place and with new people, his desire to avenge the honor of Concetta Marie was an overpowering force he felt helpless to resist. He decided on one last act of violence.

After working out a scenario by which he could punish Ettore Umberto in an appropriate manner, Salvatore started the process by walking Concetta either to or from the farm where she was working. He wanted to meet the man in question; to be able to put a face with the unspeakable acts. On one day in particular, Salvatore brought Concetta to the farm. As they walked and approached the property, Salvatore could sense the tension in his young bride to be. Her demeanor went from happy and carefree to distracted and fearful. There they saw Ettore Umberto, a menacing presence, seemingly waiting for Concetta. Umberto was short, heavy-set, with thick, dark eyebrows and coal black eyes. He wore a nondescript cap, a brown jacket, grayish trousers and he held a cane in his right hand. Salvatore maintained a hint of a smile on his face. Salvatore said hello, but Ettore Umberto only grunted. "You are late", he growled at Concetta. "Please forgive her, but she was delayed at school…" Before Salvatore could complete the sentence, Umberto snapped, "And who the hell are you?"

Unbeknownst to the fat man, his demeanor toward Salvatore was helping to seal his fate. Although Salvatore's plan was designed in such a way as to provide a cooling period, an opportunity to perhaps go in a different direction, all Umberto accomplished by his attitude that day was to set Salvatore's plan into immediate action.

Salvatore drew Concetta close and whispered in her ear. "Don't worry, he will stop pestering you soon". That was all that Salvatore said; he kissed Concetta and waved goodbye to Ettore Umberto. Salvatore's information, culled after weeks of waiting and evaluation, resulted in him learning that Ettore Umberto resided in Baselice, a few km from Foiano di Val Fortore. He also knew that Umberto had a habit of staying overnight at the farm Mondays through Fridays during the planting season. Following the Friday workday, he mounted his horse and travelled to his home in Baselice. Today was Friday.

On this day, Salvatore's plan would go into action. With Sr. Fisco bedridden, Salvatore tended to the barbershop alone. This gave him the opportunity to come and go as needed. The plan was to pick up Concetta at the farm, walk her back toward Foiano and her home, then under some pretense, return to the farm and carry out his action.

Salvatore arrived at the farm at 3 0'clock in the afternoon. He met Concetta at the entry to the property and walked her toward Foiano, about 1.5 km further. She was quiet; it had not been a good day. He stopped when they were within one half a km from home and said, "*Stupid me*. I forgot to put an extra log on the fire at the shop. I fear it will be very cold tonight, and I want the shop to be comfortable tomorrow morning. Go on ahead, and I will catch up". Concetta smiled, kissed him and continued toward the house.

Salvatore doubled back to the farm, making certain that no one saw him. He walked through the woods, which lined both sides of the road between Foiano and Baselice. He reached the point where he knew Umberto would take the road north to Baselice, a journey of about five km. He waited for approximately twenty-five minutes, concealing himself along the left side of the road; he heard the hooves of Umberto's horse coming up from the farm. He crouched down, waiting to identify the rider, make certain that he was alone and luring him into the trap that he had set for him.

The fat man bobbed along looking as if he hadn't a care in the world. Salvatore's mind raced as he thought about the indignities his fiancé had endured for many months. He thought about the fact that Concetta had no one else to turn to for justice, and that even her well-meaning father seemed unwilling or unable to settle this issue. The question in Salvatore's mind was long ago settled and the judgment day for Ettore Umberto had arrived.

As Umberto's horse lumbered along, he passed the hidden Salvatore Tegianno. Salvatore waited until the rider was beyond him; in a flash, Salvatore sprang from his place of hiding and quickly approached the horse from behind, at its left flank. Like a mountain lion, he charged the unwitting rider, grabbing his coat from behind, and then yanking him off the steed. The older man was caught completely off guard; he fell off the horse and landed hard on his left side. In one motion, Salvatore slapped the hindquarters of the horse, causing it to rear, then to bolt down the trail. In another quick motion, Salvatore was on top of Ettore Umberto, who had been on his back. Ettore's cap was partially over his eyes; Salvatore's powerful left hand was at the man's fleshy neck, both pinning him to the ground and choking him. Salvatore straddled Ettore's ample stomach, further causing distress to him.

Ettore Umberto's arms began to flail, swatting and grasping at the same time. He felt the life being choked out of him and could do nothing at all but flail. A well-timed punch, delivered straight down from short range, struck the corpulent man squarely on his nose. Soon, thick blood was oozing from the crushed appendage. As Ettore emitted gurgling sounds, Salvatore's vice-like grip on his neck increased. The victim's right hand made on last flail; Salvatore felt a sharp pain on his chin. Ettore's fingernail had gashed Salvatore, drawing blood.

Salvatore became even more enraged now. Both hands were now upon the man's throat. Ettore Umberto at last ceased flailing. As Concetta's nemesis lay still, bleeding profusely from his face, but still alive, Salvatore administered the coup d grace. Seeing a medium sized, smooth stone within a few feet of the struggle, he picked it up with his right hand and delivered a smashing, final blow, effectively caving in the left side of the man's skull.

Salvatore rose from his position atop the abuser; he instinctively looked around to see if anyone was a witness to what had transpired. Satisfied that he had accomplished his task without witnesses, he grabbed the coat collar of the man and dragged him a little further toward an outcropping of gray rocks along the left side of the road. Salvatore then turned Ettore Umberto's lifeless body on its stomach and placed his head against a large rock. Salvatore stepped back and evaluated the scene. He was satisfied that when the body was found, it would be surmised that the man was thrown from his horse, struck his head and had been killed in a tragic accident.

Salvatore walked back into town, entered the barbershop of Michele Fisco and began to clean up. He washed the blood from his hands, shook out the dust from his clothing and washed his face. He had a cover story as to why he would be late for dinner, but he needed to be able to explain the gash on his chin.

Dinnertime at the Fisco home was typical. Mama was scurrying about, putting the final touches on yet another simple but nutritious meal. As was typical, the fireplace provided lighting, warmth and was utilized to prepare much of the meal. Anthony was setting the table; Concetta was in her parent's bedroom with her bedridden father. Salvatore apologized for his tardiness.

Salvatore joined his family at the table. After grace, the plates were filled with a Fisco specialty, ceci spinaci, or chickpeas, and spinach. As Salvatore savored the delicious meal, his mind wandered back to the deed that he had done only minutes earlier. Any guilt he may have felt was washed away when he looked across the table at the still innocent face of his fiancé. She would no longer be subjected to the wanton lust of that evil man, Ettore Umberto.

"What happened to your chin?" Anthony asked, his voice laced with concern as he pointed to the fresh gash. The question caught Salvatore off guard, jolting him back to reality. He had entirely forgotten about the sharp reminder of the violence that had recently touched their lives. "Yes, I was going to ask you that too, my love. You didn't have that when I last saw you," Concetta said, her brow furrowing with worry as she reached out, her fingers gently grazing his skin as if to heal the wound with her touch. Salvatore, sensing the weight of their gazes, scrambled to concoct a plausible excuse. "I went back to the shop to keep the fire roaring and decided to shave myself. In my haste, I slipped with the blade, and, alas, I cut myself," he explained, forcing a chuckle to mask his discomfort. "I hope you don't carve up your customers like that," Mama remarked, a teasing lilt to her voice, and despite the gravity of their situation, soft laughter bubbled up, momentarily lifting the heavy atmosphere that surrounded them. Yet, the lightness was fleeting. From the bedroom came the haunting sound of Michele Fisco's cough—a harsh, gurgling noise that echoed through the small home. It was a sound the family had grown all too familiar with over the long months of witnessing his slow decline. "I wish something could be done," Anthony murmured, despair clouding his youthful eyes as tears began to glisten like fragile dew drops. "We all do, son," Mama replied, her voice heavy with sorrow. The words hung in the air like a silent acknowledgment of their shared pain. Each of them understood the harsh truth: their only option was to make Michele as comfortable as possible as they faced the inevitable.

Chapter 13:

Blowback

The two men approached the still smoldering ruins of the dwelling with caution. The odor of kerosene permeated the otherwise fresh morning air. The home that Francesco Arcuri had built and shared with his family for as long as anyone could remember was nearly gone. As a veteran member of the Arcuri crime family, Frank Nicastro felt an almost crushing sense of pressure that day. Along with fellow soldier Tomaso Contorno, he represented what was left of a powerful and influential presence in this part of Sicily for many years. With the Don eliminated and the whereabouts of his son and underboss, Giuseppe Garfagnini, unknown, a serious leadership dilemma loomed. After observing the charred remains within the house, Nicastro concluded that the leadership of the Arcuri family had been effectively decapitated in a relatively short time. Inside the ruins, there were two, possibly three, additional victims, presumably the Don's wife and children. "God. I cannot tell from this mess who, or how many, were here, can you?" muttered Contorno, sifting carefully through the debris with a tree branch. "Nor can I, Tomaso," Nicastro replied quietly and respectfully. "The revenge appears to be complete. The Don, as well as his family—all gone." Nicastro made the sign of the cross.

"But what of Salvatore?" asked Contorno. "Either he is among those lost here, or he was captured. If so, God have mercy on his soul." The older man stopped in the middle of what had been the kitchen, looking left and right as if searching for something. "Unless he escaped," Nicastro suggested, a mixture of hope and dread in his voice. The underboss could never have known how close he was to solving the riddle of "What became of Salvatore Arcuri." Although he fervently wanted to believe that the second-in-command had survived and was not captured, he struggled to accept the possibility that the family's titular leader had fled like a frightened dog. If he had run away, he would have abandoned not only his family of like-minded criminals but also his actual family. This would seem "peccaminoso" — a sinful and disrespectful act. It was both cowardly and unforgivable. As Nicastro and Contorno pondered their next move, little did they realize that one body not part of the conflagration belonged to the youngest son of Francesco Arcuri. Armando Loggia, another soldier loyal to the Arcuri family, was proud of both his loyalty to his Don and his status as a proven leader of men, respected by many. Francesco Arcuri had recognized Loggia's strength and leadership qualities early on. Over the years, these traits allowed him to rise from soldier to "Caporegime," meaning leader of the soldiers. Within the ranks of the Arcuri family, Loggia held the fourth position in terms of prestige, power, and influence.

Armando's sharp instincts had been instrumental in his ascent through the criminal ranks. They not only secured his position but also preserved his life, along with the life of the boss's youngest son. Loggia, sensing the precariousness of Francesco Arcuri's bold power play, had begun to anticipate a nightmare scenario: a failed coup that could lead to devastating fallout. This realization prompted him to devise a personal escape plan. At thirty-seven, Armando was a solitary man, a widower with no children to anchor him. He felt a certain freedom in this lack of familial ties, convinced that he could vanish if the situation demanded it. His escape route led to North Africa. Familiar with Tunisia—a captivating land not too distant from Sicily—he saw it as a refuge, far enough away to offer safety, at least until the storm passed. He had established connections at Cape Passero who could facilitate his passage across the Malta Channel into Tunis. He had meticulously arranged every detail of his flight, but his plan was singularly focused on his own escape, leaving no room for a companion. On the fateful day of the murders, Loggia had visited the Arcuri estate, guided by a nagging hunch, but he arrived too late to intervene. As he made his way down the dirt road, he stumbled upon his boss's son, a disoriented fifteen-year-old named Nico. The boy looked dazed and lost, his eyes wide with shock and sorrow, utterly unprepared for the horrific events that had unfolded at his home. Without hesitation, Armando beckoned Nico into his wagon, where the trembling teenager began to share his harrowing tale. "I was sent to fetch water," Nico recounted, his voice barely above a whisper. The creek was not far from the sprawling estate, yet it had been a sufficient distance to spare him from the marauders who had invaded his world. "It doesn't matter," Loggia reassured him, brushing a hand across the boy's shoulder. "They're gone now, I'm truly sorry to say." As the wagon creaked and rumbled onward, Nico's quiet sobs cut through the oppressive silence, each tear a reflection of his shattered life. He had no inkling that this moment marked a significant turning point in his young life. They were heading south, away from Ragusa—a place now steeped in tragedy—toward Cape Passero, and further on to the shores of Tunisia, a land brimming with new opportunities and uncertainties yet to unfold.

Chapter 14:

Marriage

The marriage of Salvatore Treggiano and Concetta Maria Fisco took place on the crisp morning of October 10th, 1894. As Salvatore made his way to the church of the Holy Rosary, he was taken aback by the large gathering of townsfolk on that clear, sunlit Autumn Day. It felt as if the entire community—approximately twelve hundred souls—had come out to commemorate this joyous occasion. Despite the recent passing of Concetta's father, a mere one and a half months prior, the atmosphere brimming with laughter and the clinking of glasses transformed the event into a celebration of life. Salvatore discerned a palpable sense of relief that washed over Concetta and her mother since the death of Sr. Fisco. They viewed it as a merciful end to a prolonged suffering, recognizing that their loved one's battle with illness had finally relinquished him from pain. In stark contrast, young Anthony, Sr. Fisco's teenage son, struggled with the grief of losing his father. Salvatore couldn't help but notice the similarities between the grieving boy and his own brother Nico—both grappling with the shadows of their loss. As his heart raced in anticipation of the wedding vows he was soon to take, Salvatore was haunted by a sense of guilt that he couldn't shake. It was as if an invisible weight pressed upon him. Deep within, he understood that the foundation of his union with Concetta was beginning under a false pretense; he was Salvatore Arcuri in truth, yet he would present himself as Salvatore Teggiano to his bride and their future children, a name steeped in deception. As the ceremony neared, a stark realization dawned on him: he could not remain in this quaint, secluded town forever as a "Povero uomo," or poor man. The letters he received from his friend Gio, an expatriate thriving in America, continuously fueled his yearning for adventure and opportunity. Although he cherished the safety of this isolated mountain village, with its rustic charm, a roof over his head in the back room of a barber shop, a radiant bride by his side, and a trade he had learned, he instinctively knew that living a life limited by poverty would not suffice for long. Complicating his emotional turmoil was the news of Concetta's pregnancy, which added layers of obligation, not only to his new family but also to her widowed mother and her son, Anthony, who might soon be bereft of both parental figures. Michele Fisco, Concetta's late father, had been haunted by ominous premonitions of his own mortality. The persistent cough and alarming blood he had expectorated led him to share his fears with Father Ionotta. Together, they quietly accepted the disheartening truth that time was slipping away, leaving Anthony unprepared to inherit his father's barbering trade. Just as despair threatened to engulf them, fortune smiled upon the town when Salvatore arrived, bringing with him the potential to alleviate their worries. In the period following Salvatore's arrival, a whirlwind of events unfolded. Was it divine providence or sheer luck that things took such a favorable turn? The townspeople often spoke of the power of prayer, particularly their devotion to Saint John, suggesting that their collective supplications had indeed elicited a positive response. As he reflected on the rapid series of occurrences since his arrival in the enchanting Fortore Valley, Salvatore was acutely aware that he stood on the precipice of formidable decisions. The wedding ceremony culminated in a lively celebration that spilled into the town square. Surrounded by tables adorned with vibrant cloths, festooned with colorful banners and fragrant flowers, Salvatore felt a wave of nostalgia wash over him. The decorations reminded him of the last grand festivity the town had experienced—the feast day in November, when joy permeated the air. The modest residents of Foiano di Val Fortore, though not affluent, had rallied together to bestow their blessings on the newlyweds through the Italian concept of "barattare," a form of barter. Instead of traditional gifts, townspeople arrived bearing an assortment of offerings—bushels of sun-ripened produce, lovingly crafted linens, and even livestock like pigs and chickens! Salvatore, initially taken aback, was profoundly moved by the depth of their generosity. Each humble gift represented not merely a transaction but the heartfelt spirit of community and shared joy, far more meaningful than any gold coin could convey. Concetta Maria Teggiano glimmered like a shining star, her beauty accentuated by her simple yet elegant white gown and delicate veil. Despite her condition, she exuded an undeniable purity, her radiant smile drawing warm embraces, soft kisses, and genuine blessings from every well-wisher. The overwhelming kindness and affection of the townsfolk felt strange yet enchanting to Salvatore, wrapping around him like a comforting embrace. Yet, beneath this newfound happiness, he understood that pressing decisions loomed in the near future. Today marked a significant turning point; the man who had once been known as Salvatore Francesco Arcuri ceased to exist. In that moment, Salvatore Teggiano emerged—a man who had embraced the responsibilities of marriage, anchored himself in his newfound community, apprenticed in a trade, and begun to establish a family. It seemed he had left behind a tumultuous past filled with crime, violence, and domination. Before him lay a future replete with unfamiliar possibilities—tranquility, stability, and the anonymity of a simple peasant life, one that came with its own set of challenges. However, Salvatore had not forgotten that an alternative path lay before him. That option, though, shimmered with the allure of adventure, accompanied by the peril of uncertainty even more profound than the life choices that led him to the untouched beauty of the Fortore Valley.

Salvatore had already decided that like Giuseppe Capuano, he would go to America.

Chapter 15:
Cape Passero

The journey to Cape Passero whisked Armando Loggia and his young companion southward, guiding them to the enchanting spot where the Ionian and Mediterranean seas kissed—a picturesque locale that the locals often romantically described. However, a bitter irony gnawed at Loggia's mind as they traveled directly toward the Province of Siracusa, the very battleground where Francesco Arcuri had plotted his ill-fated conquest. It was a tragic twist of fate that this beautiful area, which should have been a refuge, had become the epicenter of destruction where so many lives would be shattered. For Armando, the absurdity of using such a place as a launch point to escape the chaos that had erupted weighed heavily on his conscience. He was acutely aware of how perilous their situation had become. As a seasoned strategist, Armando Loggia was no stranger to the art of risk assessment. He had meticulously calculated every possible move necessary to orchestrate their escape from the relentless vengeance of the revenge squad, men whose loyalty to their boss ensured that nothing would stand in the way of their brutal mission. Armando understood well the predicament that Don Vito Pedrotti faced. The brutal murder of his family member at the hands of the Arcuris could not simply be swept aside. A man of immense power and influence, Pedrotti was notorious for his ruthlessness and would never allow himself to be perceived as weak. Retribution was not just a possibility—it was a foregone conclusion. Beside him, Nico's eyes, once red and puffy from tears, now stared blankly ahead, lost in a world devoid of everything he once held dear. The weight of sudden loss etched deep lines of sorrow on his young face, and it was evident that he was likely hungry. The rickety wagon jolted along the uneven dirt road, and Armando knew it was time to strategize once more. Their stomachs grumbled in unison, signaling the need for sustenance, and a coach stop loomed ahead. Without hesitation, Armando decided to bypass the bustling stop. "A public place would be too risky," he mused. Nico, sensing the boy's confusion, inquired, "Are we not stopping for something to eat?" With a reassuring smile, Armando replied, "I'm sure we'll find a fruit and vegetable stand soon enough." True to his word, just ten minutes later, they stumbled upon a quaint roadside stand, a colorful array of fruits on display under a sun-drenched awning. Armando skillfully guided the wagon to the side, allowing the weary horses to rest. As they disembarked, Loggia and Nico took the opportunity to stretch their cramped limbs and relieve themselves, then indulged in the sweetness of fresh oranges and ripe pears. After settling the bill with the friendly merchant, Armando asked, "Can you tell us how far it is to Cape Passero?" "Only a few kilometers," the man replied, his voice warm and inviting. Cape Passero lay perched at the southeastern tip of Sicily, a land of striking contrasts. As the wagon continued its journey, Loggia nudged Nico with his elbow, a twinkle of excitement in his eye. "Look over there, Nico," he pointed, directing the boy's gaze toward the tall, stately lighthouse that loomed over the rugged coastline, standing sentinel at the water's edge, as if guarding secrets of the past. The structure, resembling a fortified tower, captivated Nico, who had never before encountered such a magnificent sight. "We've officially arrived at our destination," Loggia announced, his voice filled with a mix of relief and anticipation. As they navigated through the streets, Nico squinted at a sign that read "Via Tonnara." With its broader thoroughfare buzzing with activity, it appeared to be the heart of the town. Small shops and stalls lined the vibrant street, their owners calling out to potential customers with enthusiasm. "What now?" Nico asked, curiosity etched on his young face. Armando, scanning the surroundings with purpose, instructed, "Keep an eye out for Via Vittoria." However, as they passed numerous shops and alleys, the sought-after street eluded them. Finally, conceding to the futility of searching, Armando pulled over to ask a local woman who was sweeping her porch. "Mi scusi, potete dirmi dove trovare via Vittoria?" The woman paused, her broom still in hand, and corrected him gently. "You mean Vittorio. Stay on this road and continue for about three kilometers…" Nico felt a flicker of hope at the woman's reassurance that they were only a short distance from their goal. His stomach grumbled audibly in agreement. After another forty minutes of travel, they reached a narrow sliver of land jutting into the sea, a wild, untamed landscape that felt almost otherworldly. Here, a row of weathered wooden shacks stood precariously close to the water's edge, their frames battered by the salty breeze. Suddenly, a figure emerged from one of the buildings, a rugged man wielding a shotgun. "What's your business here?" he barked, stepping closer, his squinting eyes narrowing with suspicion. Yet as the man approached, recognition flickered across his face. "Armando… is that you?" he asked, surprise igniting the twilight air.

Armando stepped off the wagon, and the two men embraced. "It is I," he said. "This is Nico, and I hope you will be able to accommodate him as well. I realize this was unexpected, but I am prepared to pay his fare." "Not a problem, my friend!" the man replied, suddenly cordial and helpful. Nico was greatly impressed by the fact that the Capo seemed to have friends everywhere, just like his father. Before long, the man ensured that the wagon and horses were taken care of, and that Nico and Armando were brought inside to bathe and enjoy a meal while the two older men discussed business. After the meal, Nico expected to be excluded from the conversation about the details of the rest of the journey. As he started to excuse himself, Armando ordered him back to the table. "I want you to hear this, Nico," he said calmly yet firmly. "This journey and these decisions will impact you, so it is important for you to understand the details." For Nico, who was used to being left out of "man talk" by his father and older brother, this was unexpected. Yet, for the first time in his young life, he felt important. He rejoined the table and listened intently to what was discussed. The plan outlined included passage from Porto Palo di Capo Passero to the African nation of Tunisia. For a boy who had seldom ventured beyond the confines of his native Ragusa, Nico was about to embark on the trip of a lifetime. The journey across the Mediterranean Sea would be long and arduous, but Armando assured him it was necessary. Although some details of the trip were shared with Nico, what he did not know was that the older man planned to hide and regroup in Tunisia, with the goal of returning to Sicily to rebuild the Arcuri family business. While young Nico's journey to Tunisia would be relatively straightforward and without drama, he could never imagine how his entry into America would alter his life.

Chapter 16:
Gio Establishes Himself

Gio Capuano was roused from his slumber by the enticing aroma of freshly brewed coffee wafting through the air from the kitchen of the boarding house on Birch Street. He had recently settled into the home of the Russo family, warm-hearted Italian immigrants who had made their way to America. Initially, they had landed in Ohio, but the allure of South Bethlehem's thriving job market ultimately drew them to this bustling community. The Russos had roots in Campania, and having established themselves firmly in the 1880s, they took it upon themselves to assist fellow Italians, particularly those from their own region, in navigating the unfamiliar landscape of their new homeland. As he glanced around the dimly lit bedroom he shared with two other men, Gio noted the rhythmic snoring of one of his roommates but realized it wasn't his cousin, Carlo Zollo. Rushing downstairs, Gio entered the large, bustling kitchen, where he found Carlo already seated at the sturdy wooden table, dressed in his work attire and savoring a steaming cup of coffee. "Ah, there he is!" Carlo exclaimed, waving him over. Mrs. Russo, a sturdy matron with a no-nonsense demeanor, peeked over her shoulder before asking what Gio wished for breakfast. The Italians in America communicated in a colorful mix of animated Italian and imperfect English, a blend that was helping Gio and others develop their rudimentary English skills. "Se vuoi qualcosa di speciale, dimmi!" (If you want something special, tell me!) she called out. "Otherwise, go to a restaurant!" she added with a hint of playful irritation. Gio couldn't help but chuckle at her gruff sense of humor; she clearly had little patience for catering to the whims of her boarders. He offered her a warm smile in return. As he sat down beside Carlo, Gio felt a sense of contentment wash over him. His positive outlook and firm self-confidence contributed to his overall satisfaction with his living situation. Nearly two years into his American adventure, he reflected on the rapid progress he had made—finding stable housing and securing a decent job in a place brimming with opportunities. For a man born into a life of peasantry and limited prospects, he and others from Foiano were beginning to catch a glimpse of independence and success. The American Dream, it seemed, was not just a distant fantasy for Gio, Carlo, and many others; it was within reach. After finishing their breakfast, Mrs. Russo placed three neatly folded brown paper bags on the small table by the back door. Inside were their lunches, each identical and carefully packed as always: hearty sandwiches filled with spicy salami and creamy provolone cheese, often complemented by succulent fried sweet peppers and onions. On the side, there was usually a piece of fresh fruit, perhaps an apple or a pear. The bread, a beloved staple, was homemade, and while Mrs. Russo might have been a terse landlady, she was undeniably a skilled baker. The aroma of the freshly baked bread lingered in the kitchen, a comforting reminder of the hearty meals they enjoyed every day. After donning their hats and grabbing their lunch bags, Carlo bid Gio farewell and headed south toward Packer Avenue, where he worked as a custodian at Lehigh University. Gio turned in the opposite direction, making his way toward the North Penn Rail line. The vibrant tracks snaked through South Bethlehem, with the area between Fourth Street and the river serving as a bustling transportation hub. Passenger and freight trains thundered through continuously, their whistles echoing through the air, while new electric trolleys zipped along New Street and Fourth, signaling the arrival of modernity. Gio took pride in having advanced to a more significant position than his initial menial job. As a gateman, he belonged to a small fraternity of dedicated workers who operated the crossing gates scattered across the borough, securing the thoroughfares as trains passed by. He was assigned to one of the busiest gates at Elm Street, a crucial intersection where trains frequently rumbled through. Climbing the rickety, steep staircase leading to his elevated vantage point, perched about twenty feet above the streets, he took a moment to absorb the lively scene below. At the top, he found his counterpart finishing up the night shift, a taciturn Irishman known only as "McFadden." Gio had learned little about McFadden, as the man had offered only a few short words since they first met. The Irishman's cold demeanor suggested he was not one of those eager to welcome the influx of Italians to South Bethlehem. Gio puzzled over McFadden's aloofness, considering that both were fellow immigrants; it seemed strange that McFadden would harbor such unfriendliness, especially since the Irish had settled in America decades prior. For McFadden, his people had arrived mid-century, driven by the promise of a better life. They had played a pivotal role in building the area, laboring tirelessly to dig the Lehigh Canal and construct the rail networks. Through this backbreaking work, the Irish had established themselves as the primary "nonnative" group in South Bethlehem, having founded the Catholic Church of Holy Infancy and formed the local network of shops and saloons. Their investments were woven into the very fabric of the community. Within forty years, the Irish had also become politically influential; the rise of Tammany Hall had begun to ripple through South Bethlehem, recognizing the significant numbers of not just Irish but various foreign-born workers who could be mobilized to swell the ranks of the Democratic Party, fueling the political machinery that would come to define the borough.

In his continuous effort to show friendship to the Irishman, Gio reached into his bag and offered him an apple. Unfortunately, all McFadden could smell was the strong odor of provolone cheese, which repulsed him. He brusquely brushed past Gio without a word and headed down the stairs. In his elevated position, Gio had at his disposal a chair, a kerosene lamp, a wooden control arm that allowed him to raise and lower the long wooden gate, and a telegraph connection that rang a bell signaling the approach of a train. For the next nine hours, the lives and well-being of countless pedestrians, horses, and trolleys rested in Gio Capuano's hands. Once settled in his roost, Gio had a commanding view to the north of the Lehigh Zinc Works, the iron company, the river, and atop the hill, the borough of Old Bethlehem. To the south, he could see the South Mountain and the campus of the university where his cousin worked as a custodian. His view to the east and west was unobstructed for quite some distance, provided there was no fog and the smoke from the zinc and iron plant was minimal. Gio lit a match and began puffing on a cigar. Soon after, he produced paper and a pencil. He decided to reach out to his friend, Salvatore, once again.

Chapter 17:

Finalizing a Plan

―――◆O◆―――

The anticipated conversation between Salvatore Teggiano and young Anthony Fisco took place in the barbershop in the heart of the small community. Salvatore had summoned Anthony to visit the shop after school on a crisp Tuesday afternoon, the air fragrant with the scent of aftershave and freshly brewed coffee. As the bell above the door chimed softly, Anthony stepped inside, his school bag slung over one shoulder. Salvatore was just finishing up a careful shave on Signior Esposito. Anthony's keen eyes noticed a fleeting exchange between the two men—a whispered word from Signior Esposito, a nod from Salvatore. There was an unspoken understanding between them, and Anthony's brow furrowed, sensing that the customer was pleading for a favor: *"Another deadbeat,"* Anthony thought bitterly. With the shop now empty aside from the two of them, Anthony found himself seated across from his brother-in-law. The term "brother-in-law" still felt foreign on his tongue, but he was growing accustomed to their familial bond. Salvatore insisted he be called simply by his name—no formalities necessary. Anthony appreciated this sincerity. "Please, sit, Anthony," Salvatore urged, his voice a mixture of gravity and encouragement. He removed a heavy, cast-iron pot from the stove, steam swirling around him, and poured himself a cup of rich, dark coffee. "Would you like a cup?" he offered. "No, thank you," Anthony replied, his eyes bright with curiosity. "I offered it to you because I see you more as a young man now, rather than just a boy." Flushed with pride, Anthony straightened his posture, eager for Salvatore's approval. "Anthony, I wanted to speak with you about something important—something your father wished for you to know." At these words, Anthony's heart raced, his mind suddenly alert. "You see, your father dreamed of you taking over this shop one day. Initially, he was patient, planning to guide you after your schooling. But as his illness progressed, he understood that time was not on his side," Salvatore continued, the shadows of sadness creeping into his tone. It was a revelation; Anthony had never grasped the depth of his father's concerns. "Your father didn't want to burden you, so he entrusted his knowledge to me, hoping that when the time came, I could teach you the skills you needed. He had a chilling premonition of his fate, and sadly, he was right," Salvatore said, letting the weight of his words linger in the air, waiting for a reaction from the stunned teenager. Confusion washed over Anthony's face, a myriad of questions swirling in his mind. *"Where are you going?"* he finally asked, the innocence of his query piercing through the heaviness of the moment.

Salvatore paused, taken aback by the simple, profound question. It revealed a maturity in Anthony that surpassed his years, an understanding that hinted at deeper implications. Though he had spoken the truth, Salvatore had skirted the reality of his own departure from the Fortore Valley, knowing that Anthony sensed the gravity of the situation. "What makes you ask such a question?" he replied, his voice tinged with surprise. "Because there's hardly enough work for one barber," Anthony explained, his tone edged with concern. "We only have one chair, and our family struggles to make ends meet, toiling in the fields while this shop barely provides. There's not enough for two barbers to thrive…" His astute observations were undeniably correct. Salvatore recognized Anthony's instinctive intuition, realizing that the boy could see through the veil of his unsatisfied restlessness; perhaps even the whispers of Concetta had reached him. The unspoken truth hung thickly between them, a realization that would change everything.

If Salvatore felt the need to mislead the boy, he quickly realized it would be fruitless, as Anthony was wise beyond his years. Honesty would be Salvatore's best policy. For perhaps the first time in a long while, the man who had changed his identity and fabricated numerous lies upon arriving in this place would be best served by being truthful about the next chapter of his life. Salvatore sent Anthony on his way; he needed to clear his mind and decide how to proceed. He even briefly considered postponing or even abandoning his dream of following Gio Capuano to America. His original plan had been to leave everyone and everything behind, but the death of Signor Fisco, the marriage to Concetta, and the impending birth of a child complicated that plan greatly. Because he genuinely loved Concetta, he knew he could never abandon her. The old Salvatore Arcuri might have, and probably would have, but this Salvatore Teggiano was a different type of man.

At that time, some 700 kilometers away, Nico Arcuri found himself a victim of his emotions upon arriving at Cape Passero. The sudden loss of his parents, his sister, and most likely his older brother was almost impossible to process. Armando Loggia, though fearless, highly intuitive, and even intelligent, was unable or unwilling to offer any real comfort to him. His explanation of what had happened was sparse and delivered without any real emotion. Perhaps the seeming coldness was merely a defense mechanism designed to distance him from pain and sorrow. In any case, Nico would have to bear his emotional trauma alone. "Nico? Can you join me in the kitchen?" It was Armando calling. Breakfast awaited

Nico, consisting of figs, yogurt, and a piece of bread, all washed down with fresh milk. Armando unfurled a large piece of paper. Also on the table were official-looking documents. "Passports?" Nico wondered aloud. The older man confirmed that the paperwork included passports, as well as a map and a diagram. Nico was about to receive unexpected news about the remainder of their journey. "Nico, soon we will separate," Armando said. "What? What do you mean?" asked the stunned teenager. "We are both being hunted, but I am hunted for a reason. You are an innocent victim of what has transpired," Armando began. "I, by the certain choices I have made, deserve what is happening, I suppose. I am not filled with joy, but I accept my fate."

Nico spoke, "Your fate? What do you mean by fate? I don't..." Armando interrupted him, "What I mean is that every adult who has either lost their life or is in extreme danger knows that this day might come, except for your sister. God rest her soul." "My mother too?" "She is an adult as well, so in a way, yes, she knew what could happen. Only children can be considered innocent. Unfortunately, we are dealing with vicious animals—men who would stop at nothing to achieve their goal of retribution." "I don't understand," said Nico. "Perhaps one day you will... or you won't. At any rate, I feel it's my final duty to ensure that you live long enough to sort this all out for yourself. Don't feel too bad about not understanding it." Armando folded up the papers and touched the boy's cheek. "I need you to promise me that from now on, you will trust me and accept what I have planned for you, for your own good." He then described the part of the journey designed specifically for Nico.

--- Salvatore explained to Concetta that he would be unhappy spending the rest of his life in Campania. "There is nothing here, Concetta," he said. Concetta realized her husband was right, yet she struggled to understand the logistics of the plan he revealed. She thought she heard him say that the goal of the plan was to go to America—a place she had only heard of during her time at the church school. She knew that several Foianese, most notably Gio Capuano and his cousin, had traveled to this far-off place in search of a dream. To Concetta, it sounded too distant and, in fact, impossible. Yet, she loved Salvatore and trusted his judgment. "But what about my mother and my brother?" she asked. "That's not a problem," Salvatore replied as he outlined what he believed to be a solid plan. "I will make sure that Anthony can support the family until I can send for you. I will travel to America, where a job awaits me." "Gio, I suppose, filled your head with these stories," she remarked.

"Yes. I know you think he exaggerates, but we have stayed in touch since he departed, and he has become established." Salvatore continued, "Gio has a good job and has connections. He will vouch for me and help me find work and a place to stay. He even tells me there is a small Foianese community there." Salvatore listed the names of people who had left Campania and settled in South Bethlehem, Pennsylvania. "You know the Cilento family? They are there. Also, the Lucarelli's, Paoletti's, Nicoletti's, and five of the Petrocelli's… they have all established themselves. There are masonry jobs, and some have become cobblers or barbers!" Concetta had indeed heard of these Foianese leaving. She listened as he continued.

"Look, I will become established, and I will send the money for you and our child. Meanwhile, between the money I send and Anthony running the shop, you will be taken care of. When I have settled, you will join me, and we will have a bright future. We can make money, and no longer will poverty be your fate". Salvatore had been practicing his story for some time. He could tell that he had made headway with his young bride.

"My mother, my brother, what will become of them if we both leave?"

Ah. *Now Salvatore understood Concetta's reticence.* "Of course, we will send for them eventually. I promise, my dear."

Chapter 18:

Uncertainty

By 1895, Salvatore's life had changed a lot. He was now married, and Concetta had given birth to a healthy son named Amato Salvatore. They chose Amato because Concetta liked the name, and Salvatore's name honored his father. Antoinette, Salvatore's mother, acted like a second mother to the baby. With the arrival of the baby, Salvatore decided it was wise for the family to move from the back room of the barbershop to the bigger flat owned by the Fisco family. This move allowed Mrs. Fisco to help her daughter take care of the infant. If she had any objections, she never showed them. In fact, Antoinette welcomed the chance to care for the baby, as it helped distract her from the pain of losing her husband. Anthony was getting used to being the family's breadwinner. He gladly left school and took a full-time job as a barber in the shop his father had started years ago. Business at the shop grew, likely because the townspeople wanted to support the Fisco family. The goodwill built by Michele, a respected citizen in town, was paying off. Anthony even obtained some paint and used his free time to freshen up the shop. While this was happening, Salvatore was preparing for his move to America. Both Anthony and Antoinette accepted his decision. Antoinette felt a mix of disappointment and acceptance. Women of her generation often accepted their roles in life. They believed their purpose was to have children and support their husbands. Antoinette understood her place in this. But Concetta was facing a tough situation. As a new mother, she worried about her husband leaving her to chase an uncertain dream. In her darkest moments, she thought it felt like discovering infidelity. Postpartum depression was a real issue even before it had a name. Concetta often felt sad and anxious, which led her to be melancholic. Antoinette noticed her daughter's sadness and tried to help. However, she fell back on old sayings to explain Concetta's feelings. "What will be, shall be," she would say. She encouraged prayer and faith in God, believing Saint John could bring peace. Over the years, Antoinette had seen many women deal with disappointment. Many women in Foiano accepted hardships and setbacks as part of life. They faced challenges like early widowhood or abandonment, especially as more men left for America.

Unbeknownst to the young and hopeful Concetta, over a dozen men from their quaint village had ventured into the unknown, each one promising to return or to send for their families once they had "established" themselves. Some, like the dashing Carlo Zollo and the earnest Gio Capuano, were free-spirited bachelors, while others were tethered to their homes by the delicate threads of marriage and children. Many of these men abandoned their families, leaving behind heartbroken wives and forlorn young ladies, their dreams of love and partnership shattered. Despite this grim reality, Antoinette clung to her faith and refused to believe that Salvatore—her handsome stranger—would fall into the same pattern of dishonor. She envisioned him as a man of integrity, someone destined for greatness.

As a devout woman, she wholeheartedly supported his ambitions and dreams. Meanwhile, Father Ionotta, too, grappled with acceptance.

He placed his trust in Salvatore, who vowed to bring his family to America. Salvatore had been forthright with his mother-in-law, laying out his dreams in vivid strokes, and because he included her and young Anthony in his vision, she embraced his promises with hope. "And don't you worry at all, mamma," he would gently assure her with a warm smile. "My plan, of course, includes the entire family. You and Anthony will also be brought over. You both deserve to live a better life!" As the months rolled on, the letters exchanged between Gio and Salvatore grew in frequency, each one thick with anticipation and longing. At one juncture, Salvatore expressed an eagerness that sparked a fire in Gio's heart: he was ready, ready to embark on his journey to America. "I have no doubt that I can secure a good job for you," Gio wrote enthusiastically, his pen gliding across the paper like the dreams dancing in his mind. "I am close to securing you a place to live. Fortune smiles upon me, and I might be able to get you into the very house where I reside. But you must act swiftly; time is of the essence, come soon!" For his part, Salvatore felt as though he had carefully woven together the strands of his new life in this adopted town.

He had crafted a new identity, nestled himself within the warmth of a family, and, in a twist of fate, married a remarkable woman—though that had not originally been part of his plan. Yet above all, he felt a triumphant sense of survival, having cheated death itself. The bitter regrets surrounding the tragic events that led to his family's demise and the collapse of his business had faded into mere shadows, dimly lit by the passing of time. The reckless decision that had sent his life spiraling into chaos was now but a distant memory. Yet the notion that Salvatore Teggiano could carve out a place for himself in America as an honorable immigrant, yearning only to embrace a life defined by dignity and lawfulness, hung in a delicate balance. What path would he tread upon arriving in this new land filled with promise? Gio, an honorable man with a heart of gold, spoke of the tremendous opportunities awaiting them—blessings tailored for men like him. But for Salvatore, the echo of his past loomed large. He was an Arcuri, a name steeped in uncertainty. The notion of contentedly settling as a humble barber or subservient employee felt stifling. Surely, the streets of America brimmed with tantalizing prospects beyond the law, didn't they?

In the far south of Sicily, Armando Loggia finalized plans, including those to send young Nico Arcuri away to safety. While part of him felt trepidation about orchestrating an uncertain future for the surviving son of Il Leone, he understood that protecting the boy was expected of him, especially as a Caporegime. Armando handed Nico a leather pouch containing transit paperwork, which would be crucial should authorities in Tunis have any questions. There was also a passport inside, necessary for the journey to America. Armando repeated several important instructions to Nico. "You are to go directly to the travel ministry located at La Goulette. Ask to see Kaled Maruani and hand him this envelope while mentioning your name." Nico nodded, his mind spinning. Armando continued, "He will open the envelope, examine the document, and then ask a simple question: 'Who is your friend?'" "Then simply tell him my name but say it this way: *Armando Pietro Loggia.*" Nico wondered why it was important to use Loggia's middle name. "It is critical that you say it exactly this way!" Armando urged. "Otherwise, he won't know we are connected. What he is allowing us to do can put all of us in great danger, even him. Do you fully understand?" Nico promised that he understood. He sensed that Loggia, a serious man, would never take these precautions unless necessary. "Good," Armando said, patting Nico on the shoulders. "There is money in the bag. I trust there will be enough to cover your journey. One more thing, Nico..." He paused as Nico looked into Loggia's dark eyes, anticipating what would come next. "When you arrive in New York City at the place called Ellis Island, you will be processed. A man named D'Angelo will be there with instructions to assist you further." "D'Angelo," Nico repeated. The older man then spent nearly an hour advising Nico on everything from how to stay safe on the ship to maintaining a low profile. "No one will know you over there. You'll have a chance to start a life," he explained. Armando deliberately did not say, "begin a new life," because he truly believed that this young man was beginning a new chapter in America. He had a unique opportunity to leave behind uncertainty and the threat of an early death. Any real uncertainty lay with Armando Loggia, who would regroup and then decide whether he had the resolve to continue the war initiated by Salvatore Arcuri.

Chapter 19:

Lombardia

Salvatore Teggiano arrived in Naples in 1895. The journey covered nearly one hundred kilometers and felt never-ending. He swore that if he were blessed to live for one hundred years, he would never again take such an arduous wagon ride. Once he disembarked, he grabbed his bags and stretched his legs. As described to him by Gio Capuano, he saw the Bay of Naples for the first time, including the mountain island of Ischia, as well as Testaccio and Burano. The harbor itself seemed enormous, and Salvatore estimated it to be over 200 hectares. He was greatly impressed by the sheer number of wharves. Fortunately, he had information about which dock to find his steamship, named "The Lombardia." This vessel was relatively new, having been launched in 1890. Salvatore was eager to depart; he could not feel truly safe until he was sailing across the Atlantic Ocean. During his time in the hidden village of Foiano di Val Fortore, he had developed a genuine sense of security. Here, however, so close to Sicily in a busy port city, he was unsure of who he might encounter or, worse still, who might recognize him. After all, the killer of his father was based nearby. As Salvatore approached the great ship, he noticed he would have plenty of company. There were long lines of people, all Italians from various regions of southern Italy and Sicily. He heard different dialects, which confirmed this to him. With a satchel in each hand and his paperwork clenched between his teeth, he finally boarded without delay. After stowing his belongings, he chose a spot on the starboard side of the Lombardia. As the ship set sail, Salvatore contemplated the fourteen-day (more or less) journey ahead and his entry into a new land. The voyage to America was straightforward and relatively uneventful. There was a brief scuffle between two men over a woman, but that was rare. Generally, the Italians were respectful of one another. Salvatore was curious about the people on board. He noticed a few obviously single young men like himself, but there were more women than he expected, and many were accompanied by young children. He began to wonder whether he should have allowed Concetta and the baby to travel with him. He quickly corrected that thought, reasoning that it would have been a mistake. After all, he needed to acclimate to this new place, which included securing a proper home for three, as well as establishing a trade. It would take time to set up a family to take advantage of the opportunities that awaited him in a land of such wealth. Much of Salvatore's time on the ship was spent crafting a plan for his arrival in America. His correspondence with Gio Capuano had led him to believe that there would be ripe opportunities to establish an American version of what his father had built in Ragusa, Sicily. The concept of protection and related rackets was an old one, certainly applicable in another country, even one so far away. Through Gio, Salvatore learned that South Bethlehem had prostitution and forms of gambling. That would be a good start. Surreptitiously—since Gio had no knowledge of Salvatore's criminal past—he inquired about the authorities, such as the police and the law, as well as whether any criminal organizations existed in that area. Convinced that there were no established crime families, Salvatore relied on his experience and instinct about human behavior to deduce that the law and police could be circumvented. As Ill Leone often said, "Ogni uomo ha il suo prezzo," or

"Each man has his price." He believed he could coerce and bribe his way into power. As Salvatore developed his plan further, he concluded it would be wise to appear as a legitimate citizen to deflect any suspicion regarding his activities.

A small, modest private venture would serve him well, but what could it be? He thought about Don Pedrotti, who hid in plain sight by posing as a humble vendor of fruits and vegetables. Regardless of how he felt about the man who had murdered his father and family, Salvatore recognized brilliance when he saw it. He decided to present himself as a respectable merchant. Ironically, he settled on the idea of opening and operating a barber shop. Through his letters with Capuano, he also learned that a potential challenge in establishing a business in South Bethlehem could have a surprising remedy. By a stroke of good fortune, he discovered through Gio that the immigrants from Foiano had the foresight to establish what they called the "Società di Mutuo Soccorso," or Mutual Aid Society. Gio explained that the purpose of this organization was to assist the Foianese in adapting to America by helping them obtain passports, steamship tickets, advice, and even loans. Salvatore's attention was particularly drawn to the notion of "loans." This plan seemed promising.

Chapter 20:
Two Journeys to America

The two-week voyage across the North Atlantic unfolded with a surprising serenity. Fortuitously, Salvatore's journey aligned with the propitious winds of November, when the gales favored travelers across the frosty ocean. As the Lombardia cut through the waves, Salvatore's heart raced with anticipation to disembark at Ellis Island and embrace his new life in America. Thanks to his friend Gio Capuano, Salvatore harbored a fair understanding of what lay ahead. Gio had informed him that the processing at Ellis Island could stretch to three or even four hours for a solitary traveler, longer for families. As the ship approached New York harbor, a sense of wonder swept through the immigrants as they caught their first glimpse of the city and the towering Statue of Liberty. her torch held high, symbolizing hope and freedom. Salvatore felt a swell of admiration for the statue, though the sight of the processing center's unremarkable wooden structures left him underwhelmed. He had imagined something grander for such an iconic entryway to a new world. Those fortunate enough to travel in first class were swiftly waved through the process, while passengers like Salvatore, categorized as third-class, faced rigorous medical and legal scrutiny upon arrival. The brisk

November winds nipped at their faces as the immigrants trudged from the dock towards the Great Hall, their breath visible in the chilly air. Inside the cavernous space, an orchestra of voices rose in a tumult, predominantly in Italian, mingled with the abrupt and often harsh sounds of English—a language foreign to many. An Italian-speaking man in a crisp uniform announced, "Se parli solo Italiano, vieni qui…"— "If you speak only Italian, come here." Eagerly, Salvatore grasped his baggage tighter and made his way through the throng, seeking solace among fellow Italians. The medical examinations were daunting, designed to detect any signs of illness lurking beneath the surface. Salvatore watched in confusion as the doctor engaged him in a curious test involving puzzles and cubes. "What is this nonsense?" he wondered, feeling a mix of bewilderment and anxiety. Following the medical checks, the legal inquiries began—questions about identity, residence, purpose, and funds. With a mix of hope and apprehension, Salvatore fabricated his name and hometown, claiming to be Salvatore Teggiano from Campania/Benevento. When asked about his financial situation, he replied cautiously, "Not too much, but I am hopeful things will change here." The official chuckled, and when asked if he had a sponsor, Salvatore confidently stated yes, naming Giovanni Capuano. He received a slip of paper and was instructed to wait on the opposite side of the hall. As he waited, Salvatore kept a vigilant ear open, noting the distressed faces of many who were not as fortunate. Some were delayed for various health concerns; any hint of tuberculosis, diphtheria, poor eyesight, or signs of mental illness could spell disaster—detention, rejection, and perhaps a return to the tumult of their homeland. He watched with a heavy heart as those who appeared distraught or tearful faced ominous news, knowing their dreams were slipping further from reach and that they might endure another fourteen days at sea. Spotting a sign reading "Area di attesa," Salvatore confirmed his directions and settled into a rickety wooden chair, feeling the weight of uncertainty pressing down on him. According to Gio, this would be the place where he would find his friend once more.

Meanwhile, unbeknownst to Salvatore, his brother Nico was also on his way to America. Each Arcuri brother, under the shadow of despair, believed the other had perished and had no inkling they were bound for the same destination. Nico's journey took an unexpected detour when his ship made an unplanned stop in Providence, Rhode Island. Naive and unable to communicate in English, Nico unwittingly disembarked at the wrong port, leaving the man waiting for him in New York puzzled and increasingly anxious. Alone and filled with trepidation, Nico's heart raced. He searched desperately for his contact, and finally, in a moment of vulnerability, he approached a sympathetic woman for help. Angelina Petrucelli, herself an immigrant and charwoman at the port terminal, noticed the panic etched on the boy's face. Setting aside her mop and bucket, she listened attentively as Nico recounted his journey, piecing together the confusion of his arrival. While she sought to comfort him, the steamship, oblivious to Nico's plight, sailed away, heading toward New York. Angelina felt an immediate surge of empathy for the frightened young man. With gentle reassurance, she placed her arm around his shoulders and guided him to a row of wooden benches, offering him a moment of refuge from his anxiety. As their conversation unfolded, Angelina discovered that Nico was a bright and capable young man. When he revealed the contents of his bag, it became apparent that he was no stowaway but rather a hopeful immigrant with all the necessary documents and carefully written instructions for navigating his entry into the United States. "I see that you seem to have all of the documents to enter this country," she said softly, inspecting his papers. Feeling a surge of compassion, she soon returned with something to eat, hoping to ease his troubled heart.

As Nico sat at the makeshift dining area in the bustling immigration center, picking at the sparse meal before him, Angelina's mind raced with determination. "Wait here," she instructed with urgency, glancing back over her shoulder. The gravity of the moment hung in the air as she contemplated her next steps. "Come ti chiami?" she asked, her voice a blend of curiosity and concern. "Mi chiamo Nico... Nico Arcuri," he replied softly, his eyes darting nervously around the room. Angelina strode purposefully toward the large, solid oak desk where the immigration officials were processing newcomers. The noise of the bustling hall filled her ears, each voice a reminder of the many hopes and dreams on the verge of being realized. Her eyes skimmed across the crowd of stern-faced men, searching intently for one specific figure among them. At the far-right corner of the desk, she spotted him—the man she hoped could help her young compatriot. Although Angelina was articulate in English, she knew that the conversation with the immigration officials would unfold in her native Italian, a language that sounded like home amidst the chaos. Pietro Donnangelo, the immigration officer she had come to trust, was the beacon of hope in this overwhelming environment. He had been her ally years ago when she first stepped onto American soil, full of dreams and anxiety. Arriving in 1889, Angelina had traversed the perilous journey from Sicily to the shores of America. Although her roots were in the western province of Trapani, she felt an instant bond with Nico. She could only hope that Pietro—being a Sicilian himself—would show the same kindness and understanding he had extended to her. Pietro was a slender man, around forty-five years old, with graying sideburns that framed his face, adding to his air of authority. His upright posture and confident demeanor earned him respect among his peers at the entry point. Known for his policy of "tough yet fair," he was a stickler for the rules, especially regarding health standards. Yet, he also believed strongly in the vital importance of sponsorship. "Do you have a sponsor?" was the question he would often ask, understanding through experience that an immigrant's success in a formidable place like Providence hinged on having someone to rely on. The importance of "vouching" for an immigrant shaped their chances of being welcomed. Although it wasn't a guaranteed ticket to prosperity, it was a crucial factor in an often unforgiving environment for those arriving from rural Italy. The transition from their agrarian roots to the frenetic pace of a rapidly industrializing city was bound to bring about a profound "culture shock" for unsuspecting immigrants. While some brought along skills in trades like masonry or cobbling, the majority landed as "unskilled and uneducated," ill-equipped to navigate the complexities of their new world. The obstacle was even greater for those with limited English proficiency, as their chances of success dwindled. As Angelina passionately articulated her case for Nico, Pietro's gaze shifted to him, the young man's face etched with uncertainty. His gaunt features and troubled expression spoke volumes about the burden he carried. Beside him lay a pair of well-worn bags, likely containing all his worldly possessions—a collection of dreams and remnants of his past life. Pietro could not help but think of the countless faces he had seen over the years at this very port, each one bearing their own stories, aspirations, and fears. "What makes this case any different?" he mused silently. But then, Pietro met Angelina's hopeful eyes, her earnest expression compelling him to reconsider. Her deep empathy resonated within him, serving as a stark reminder of the humanity behind the statistics and regulations. Turning back to Nico, Pietro prepared to speak. "Of course, I can at least start the processing and ask some fundamental questions," he began, his voice measured but approachable. "Assuming he is as healthy as he appears, and considering that the individual who would vouch for him is so far away in New York, how do you propose we address this crucial question of sponsorship, my dear Angelina?" A slight smile softly illuminated his features, suggesting a willingness to bend the rules. *"Why, of course, I would advocate for Nico,"* she replied, her voice steady and resolute. In that moment, although she had no concrete plan, a deep intuition propelled her forward, pushing her to make a promise to this young stranger whose fate was now intertwined with hers. For Nico Arcuri, who had begun his journey in a state of despair and uncertainty, a crucial turning point had just surfaced in the tumult of his new life in America. For the first time in many dark days, Nico sensed that perhaps fortune had finally begun to smile upon him.

At the bustling location of Ellis Island, Giovanni Capuano scanned the vast expanse of the main hall. There were countless people, including the immigrants being processed. Drawing from his own experience, Gio knew where to start looking for Salvatore. Optimistic about his chances of passing the initial entry tests, he instinctively headed toward the area designated by officials for immigrants needing a sponsor. Salvatore spotted Gio first. "Giovanni. Sono qui." The two men embraced, and Gio felt genuine happiness at seeing his friend. In contrast, Salvatore, a man skilled at exploiting others, saw only an opportunity. "Gio, I'm so glad to see you." Gio, bubbling with enthusiasm, talked non-stop about America and its opportunities. He boasted about his progress achieved in such a short time. "I have a place to live, an important job that pays well, and I've already saved a nice amount of money," he proclaimed. As they approached the intake area, presumably to finalize the processing, Salvatore listened to Gio's enthusiastic account of his support for this fine citizen, smiling to himself and thinking, "If any of these fools knew the truth about me, they would be locking the door instead of opening it." The door swung wide open, thanks to Gio's passionate speech about his wonderful and decent young friend. As far as the immigration officials were concerned, they were convinced that Salvatore Teggiano was a clean-cut, healthy, ambitious young man ready and willing to contribute to society in his new country. In reality, Salvatore was neither able nor willing to start fresh. Instead, his goal was to transplant his old life and knowledge to America and create a new "family business" in South Bethlehem, Pennsylvania.

Chapter 21:
Establishment in South Bethlehem

Months slipped by like grains of sand, and the little village of Foiano di Val Fortore remained untouched by any news from distant America. Anthony Fisco, now a young man of sixteen, had firmly established himself as the barber of the town, his hands deftly wielding scissors and razors. Though he had yet to hone the finer skills of a surgeon, the townspeople regarded him as a competent heir to his father's legacy. Antoinette Fisco, embodying the resilience of her generation, accepted her life's course with quiet dignity, her unwavering Roman Catholic faith, and daily prayers to Saint John the Hermit offering her solace. Yet, among them, only Concetta Maria Treggiano wore a shroud of persistent sorrow. Concetta's melancholia deepened with each passing day, entwined with the haunting possibility that the love she had surrendered to had vanished without a trace—leaving her abandoned and alone with their child.

"How could I have succumbed so profoundly to a man who could so easily walk away from us?" she lamented, tears streaming down her cheeks as she confided in her mother. Mrs. Fisco strained to defend the character of her missing son-in-law, but with each week that drifted by in silence from America, Concetta's fears loomed ever larger. "I refuse to believe that Salvatore has deserted you, my daughter. It pains me to think he would deceive the three of us," she reassured, though a flicker of doubt lingered in her heart. "Your brother believes just as I do—that Salvatore will honor the promise he made." Antoinette longed to cling to hope, but she steeled herself for the possibility of heartbreak as her days ebbed into a routine of household management and caring for her daughter's increasingly fragile spirit.

Meanwhile, at Union Station in South Bethlehem, Gio Capuano hurriedly grabbed his friend's bags, ushering him off the bustling train platform. As the clock struck four in the afternoon, the station buzzed with the vibrant energy of newcomers and locals alike. Gio, with a genuine smile, turned to Salvatore. "I trust you found the journey from New York to be rather pleasant?" "It was far more comfortable than the trip across the ocean," Salvatore replied, downplaying the restlessness of his long voyage. "Excellent! We're just a brief stroll from my home. I hope you don't mind walking," Gio explained, his enthusiasm infectious. "Not at all," Salvatore responded, taking up one of the bags as they set off together, bracing against the cold, gray embrace of the November air. As they traversed the streets towards their destination, Salvatore's eyes widened in awe at the sights and sounds of South Bethlehem, Pennsylvania. He had never encountered such a cacophony of life; men, women, and children bustling about, their faces a mix of determination and routine. The air thrummed with the rhythmic clatter of horse-drawn wagons accompanied by the high-pitched whine of an industrialized world. In the distance, train whistles pierced the atmosphere, and the resounding clang of a bell caught his attention. It was a sound he had never known—attached to a remarkable contraption that moved along metal tracks beneath a web of electrified wires.

"Cos'e?" Salvatore exclaimed, instinctively stepping back to avoid the whirling trolley car that zipped past him. "Ha!" Gio chuckled, entertained by his friend's innocent wonder, the contrast between their worlds stark and vivid in that bustling moment.

"That's the trolley. It's a way for you to get across town. I will eventually explain all the mysteries of this place to you." Gio continued, "By the way, if you notice that people refer to me as 'John', that's alright. I have adjusted my name." "Adjusted my name?" What did that mean? Of course, Salvatore had "adjusted" his own name, changing it from Arcuri to Teggiano, so perhaps he shouldn't judge too harshly. The man with the new name continued, "You see, in this country, it can sometimes be helpful to, as they say, become Americanized." Salvatore listened attentively. "A few have even changed their surnames, making them less Italian and more 'Medigan.'" Salvatore resisted the urge to criticize such a decision, for obvious reasons.

Following close behind his host and guide, Salvatore arrived at "435 Vine Street." It was a tree-lined street featuring mostly houses. Unlike the dwellings in Sicily and Foiano, these homes appeared new. Most were made of brick and were attached to one another. Directly across the street was an enormous structure. "John" informed him that it was a school. "I didn't mention in our last correspondence that I have a new and better job, and as a result, I've acquired a different place to live," John Capuano said as he produced a key from his pocket, attached to many others. He opened the front door and said, "Welcome to your new home!" A new name, a new home, a different job… What other surprises were in store for Salvatore? As one might expect, the home on Vine Street was sparsely appointed, which is typical of a bachelor's residence. Salvatore noticed that his footsteps echoed on the bare hardwood floors in the parlor and into the kitchen. There were two chairs, a small table, and a portrait on one wall of the parlor. Salvatore recognized it as Saint John. Around the wooden frame was a devotional scapular. He had learned while in Foiano that Gio, now John, was quite devout in his religious beliefs. For the first time, he wondered whether his friend had adopted the name of his favorite saint.

In the kitchen, John set a pot of water to boil. The rhythmic sound of bubbles popping filled the air, creating a soothing backdrop as he poured steaming cups of tea. "What do we have here?" Salvatore inquired, a hint of surprise in his voice, taken aback by this unexpected choice of beverage. "I've begun to embrace several American habits," John replied, a hint of pride in his tone. "Tea. It has a delightful taste, and I've been told it's quite good for you. Go ahead, enjoy." Salvatore cautiously took a sip, his expression betraying a lack of enthusiasm, yet he offered a polite thank you in appreciation of his host's gesture. "Here, you will have your own room," John declared, his chest puffed with pride. "But Gio, you mentioned sharing a room in someone's home just a while back…" Salvatore responded, skepticism creeping into his voice. With a warm smile, John Capuano explained, "I have come a long way since those days. Remember when I told you I found a better job?" Salvatore nodded, recalling their conversations. "I've saved some money and even borrowed a little more from the Società di Mutuo Soccorso. So, I managed to rent this lovely place from an Italian family. They will eventually allow me to buy and own it," John elaborated, his eyes sparkling with ambition. As Salvatore listened, he couldn't help but admire the impressive strides his friend had made in less than two years. "If a man like him can achieve so much, then surely, I should be able to find success as well," he mused to himself. However, the wheels of his mind began to turn, and Salvatore, ever the cold and calculating strategist he was, started to weave a new scheme for a "front" for his illicit activities, with John Capuano unwittingly cast in a supporting role. ---

Angelina Petrucelli resided in a modest flat on the bustling Canal Street, right in the heart of Providence's industrial hub. Just a few blocks from her workplace, the street was a labyrinth of narrow winding alleys and haphazardly laid paths that had sprung up almost organically, devoid of any careful urban planning. For an American city, Providence exuded a sense of history, having been founded in the seventeenth century by the visionary Puritan Roger Williams. This storied past seemed to cast a spell on the area, where the streets felt almost European in their erratic layout; few intersected at precise right angles, most meandering as if they had once been nothing more than well-trodden cow paths. The city, alive with activity, had burgeoned rapidly and still showed signs of growth, attracting workers from across Europe drawn by its myriad job opportunities in industries ranging from maritime trades to manufacturing, machinery, tools, silverware, jewelry, and textiles. At this point, Providence buzzed with a population of approximately 150,000, and Nico found himself awestruck by the sheer number of souls packed into this vibrant place. Angelina shared her cramped abode with her brother, Marco. The flat, consisting of three tightly knit rooms, felt intimate yet confined, but Nico was grateful for the sanctuary it provided. Under these circumstances, he could at least begin to sift through the chaos of recent events, attempting to forge a plan for his uncertain future. As he pondered, a name surfaced in his mind: D'Angelo, a man waiting for his arrival in New York. According to Armando Loggia, D'Angelo would take care of him. Yet, now, in this unexpected haven called Providence, Nico understood that he might need to reevaluate everything he thought he knew about his journey ahead.

The Italian immigrants welcomed their fellow newcomers with genuine empathy and kindness. Angelina stepped up to make Nico feel at ease in this unfamiliar environment. Having moved to America just six years earlier herself, she fondly remembered the feelings of uncertainty and anxiety that came with navigating a new language, customs, and the bustling pace of city life.

After settling in, Angelina approached Nico with warmth. "I can relate to how overwhelming it must feel right now. Please know that you're welcome to stay with us for as long as you need, and I'll do everything I can to support you," she said, her voice soothing, and the sincerity in her dark, expressive eyes spoke volumes. There was an undeniable strength in her demeanor that Nico couldn't help but appreciate and draw comfort from. Angelina's brother also offered a warm welcome, showcasing his own eager willingness to embrace their new guest. Marco was even heard enthusiastically discussing potential job opportunities for Nico, indicating his genuine desire to help him find his footing. Feeling a blend of gratitude and exhaustion, Nico thanked everyone and retreated to the cozy corner of the flat that had been quickly prepared for him. Although sleep eluded him, he felt reassured by the kindness surrounding him.

Meanwhile, Salvatore's journey in South Bethlehem began with the support of his friend, John Capuano, who was eager to help him connect with the local community. One of John's top priorities was introducing Salvatore to the Società di Mutuo Soccorso, a vibrant Foianese gathering place situated in a modest building on Mechanic Street. As they entered, Salvatore was invited to wait at a small wooden table, where he noticed Italian men engaged in lively conversations, many savoring their pipes or cigars, a few playing card games. The rich aroma of tobacco swirled around him, mingling with another enticing scent that he couldn't quite place—perhaps something delicious was cooking, like fresh fish. To his right was a bustling bar where men gathered, drinks in hand. Behind the counter stood a stocky man with a white shirt and a prominent mustache. John quickly sought out this individual, and after a brief exchange, he turned to Salvatore and pointed him out, signaling that he would be introduced shortly. The stocky man disappeared for a moment, and John returned with two glasses in hand. He sat down and presented a glass of Grappa to Salvatore with a gleam of excitement in his eye. "*You're about to meet Signor Alex Fattore,*" he said, lowering his voice as if sharing a delightful secret. "He rarely meets anyone before noon, but I've built some respect around here," John added proudly. As Salvatore took a sip of the Grappa, he found it a little too potent for his taste and set it aside, intrigued but cautious. "So, tell me about this, Fattore. Is he some sort of big deal?" Salvatore asked, curiosity sparking in his tone. The atmosphere buzzed with the promise of new friendships and the excitement of fresh opportunities, painting a hopeful picture for their future in this new land.

"My friend, I'll advise you to be most respectful of Signior Fattore for he controls whether you receive a loan, and how much". John gulped the rest of the Grappa. "Will you be wanting to finish yours?" Salvatore slid the glass toward John.

John sipped and continued. "Getting you this introduction was hard. He does this as a favor to me. Ingratiating yourself to him will, *how we say*… get your foot in the door".

For Salvatore, a man unaccustomed to kowtowing to anyone, this was demeaning. Yet, he had to come to the realization that for now, he may need to play this game. Just then, the bartender approached the table.

"Lui ti vedra ora" *He will see you now.*

Once inside the office of Signior Fattore, the formal introduction took place. "Signior, this is the friend that I have been telling you about. His name is Salvatore Teggiano, and he is from our home, in Foiano".

Salvatore instantly noticed how Capuano's approach became one of a supplicant.

"Foiano?" The man, about sixty years of age was seated behind a desk, behind small mountains of paper. He held a cigar in his left hand and a glass of Grappa in the other.

He eyed Salvatore suspiciously and snarled, *"He is no more Foianese than the Irish pig who walks the beat on the street outside"*. John was slightly taken aback; Salvatore's blood began to boil. *"Who was this little man to say this about me?"*

"I am away from Campania for many years, but I do remember all of the village's surnames and I know of no one there by such a name". Fattore continued. "Are you daring to deceive me Sr. Capuano?"

John thought quickly; he began to perspire, possibly due to the harsh words, mostly because of the effects of the powerful beverage.

"No, no, Signior, I assure you that no deception was intended. Salvatore came to the commune as a visitor and became, *how you say*, one of us. And of all things, the highly respected Father Ionotta accepted him into our town…" John looked carefully at the man, seeking a sign that he had provided a satisfactory answer.

After a long pause, Signior Alex Fattore, stood up, smiled and let out a hearty laugh. He stared directly at Salvatore and said, "As you can see, some men are easily intimidated… welcome to South Bethlehem". Fattore extended his hand to Salvatore.

As he shook hands with Signior Alex Fattore, Salvatore wondered why he would embarrass John in this fashion. He deduced that Alex Fattore was a man who needed to bluster to make himself feel superior to others. "Small pond...big fish", he reasoned. Instead of coming away in awe or with respect, Salvatore made note that this so called "big shot" was nothing of the sort and that he could likely be flattered, then taken advantage of.

The outcome of this morning's meeting with the secretary-treasurer of the Societa di Mutuo Soccorso was quite enlightening. The organization is primarily focused on offering loans to those who are settling here from Foiano, with a commitment that doesn't extend to others. While there are additional benefits to being a member, Salvatore found that access to capital stood out as the most appealing aspect. For him, this opportunity represented a pragmatic approach, much like other choices he had made throughout his life. With a modest investment in membership dues, he felt he was gaining an invaluable advantage in his ambition to carve out a niche in a new enterprise—albeit a criminal one. It's important to note that much of the initial funding for Salvatore's venture would come from the hardworking and innocent immigrants from Foiano di Val Fortore. With a combination of charm and strategic thinking, Salvatore Teggiano began to lay the groundwork for what would eventually grow into a significant criminal operation in his newly adopted hometown. South Bethlehem, during this transformative period in the late nineteenth century, was experiencing a remarkable boom. What had once been a collection of serene farms was rapidly evolving into a vibrant center of industry, a hallmark of the Industrial Revolution. The Moravians, who had previously held the lands south of the Lehigh River, had to surrender their properties during a tough economic period known as "The Panic of 1837." This hardship, lasting about six years, stemmed from various economic shifts, including a collapse in crop prices. In place of the old farmlands, there soon arose an intricate system of canals and railways vital for trade and transport. The discovery of anthracite coal and advancements in zinc smelting and eventually iron manufacturing paved the way for South Bethlehem to become a hub of business and a beacon for job seekers drawn to the new industrial age. The area's population tripled as enthusiastic entrepreneurs and hopeful workers flocked to the region, transforming it into a bustling metropolis. By 1890, South Bethlehem had grown larger and more pivotal than its older neighbor to the north, establishing a dynamic business district filled with a variety of enterprises—some of which might make the more conservative northern Bethlehem residents raise an eyebrow. It was clear that the momentum for further growth was strong, and individuals like Salvatore Teggiano recognized the potential. While many entrepreneurs were focused on traditional ventures like haberdasheries, grocery stores, barber shops, and harness-making, Salvatore envisioned unique opportunities within what might be called "vice industries." He had a keen understanding of human nature and sensed that there was ample demand for activities such as gambling and other services that would cater to the interests of the community residing on the gritty side of the Lehigh River. He astutely recognized that these ventures were as vital as any legitimate business. After his meeting with Signior Alex Fattore, the guardian of finances at the Societa di Mutuo Soccorso, and leveraging his sharp intellect against the unsuspecting John Capuano, Salvatore successfully persuaded his landlord and friend to leave his railroad job behind. Together, they agreed to open a fruit and vegetable stand at the Municipal Market along Third Street. Here, Salvatore anticipated the chance to run a business "in plain sight," strategically channeling any illicit earnings through a seemingly legitimate operation. A grocery store made perfect sense; regardless of the economic climate, food is a necessity, ensuring a consistent clientele while drawing less scrutiny. With his strategic discussions with both John Capuano and the man in charge of the Societa, Salvatore was on the right track toward achieving his goals. Now, it was time to reach out with a letter to Foiano di Val Fortore, further paving the way for his ambitions.

Chapter 22:

Nico Blossoms

The lives of the people in Foiano di Val Fortore have long been closely intertwined with the rhythms of the agricultural calendar, a tradition that has flourished in the beautiful Campania region for centuries. The community has always embraced the land's needs, especially during the bustling months from March to May, when many residents—primarily working for the prosperous padrones—dedicated themselves to preparing the fields for planting. This critical period involved intensive labor, requiring significant physical endurance, as men worked diligently with the aid of oxen and horses to till the soil. Once the groundwork was laid and the soil enriched with fertilizer, the planting began—a task often assisted by women, who also took care of the newborn animals that joyfully arrived in the early spring.

In March 1896, an air of excitement swept through Foiano with the arrival of a highly anticipated letter. The postmaster knew how much this correspondence, expected "from America," meant to the families awaiting news. Every week brought family members visiting the post office, eagerly asking if the letter had come, only to be met with a gentle,

"Sorry...no." But that day was different. The postmaster, a devoted man named Lanzetti, gripped the envelope tightly and hurried up the hill to the Fisco home. Antoinette Fisco was tending to her chickens when he finally caught his breath and exclaimed, "Finamente, una lettera dall' America!" With that, Signora Fisco clutched her chest in disbelief. Concetta, hearing the commotion, dashed to the door with her son, her face alight with curiosity and excitement. "What is it?" she said as she rushed toward Lanzetti, her smile bright like the sun. "It just arrived—I can hardly believe it! I promise I wasted no time..." he began, but his words faded as Concetta eagerly took the letter from his hands, pressing it to her heart, emotions swirling within her. "Grazie Sig. Lanzetti... Un sogno è stato esaudito..." (My dream fulfilled...) she whispered, her voice filled with hope. "Or perhaps a prayer has been answered," her mother corrected gently, sharing in the joy of the moment.

Seated at the kitchen table, Concetta felt a surge of anticipation as she opened the envelope and began to read: *"My dearest Concetta Maria, I realize that it has been far too long since my last letter. Life here has been a whirlwind as I work to establish myself, and I didn't wish to raise your hopes without good news. But now I can share that Gio and I have begun organizing our life here in South Bethlehem. It's a fascinating place, so different from the beauty of our beloved Campania or Sicily."*

"The town is wonderfully diverse, filled with people from various backgrounds. The Italians, especially our Foianese community, truly support one another, creating such a warm and friendly atmosphere. I want to give a special shoutout to Gio, who now calls himself John—he's been an absolute gem! We're living together and embarking on an exciting adventure: starting our very own fruit selling business! There's even plenty of space in my house for you, your mother, and Anthony if he decides to join us on this journey. I'm wrapping up a few things on my end, but I promise you this: very soon, I'll bring you here, where we can create a joyful life together."

This letter brought tears of joy to Concetta's eyes, and her mother felt deeply touched too. Salvatore ended his heartfelt letter with: "Credimi quando ti dico quanto ti amo e quanto mi manchi." "Believe me when I tell you how very much I love you and miss you."

In the spring of 1896, in Providence, Rhode Island, Nico Arcuri began an exciting new chapter at the Law Office of Michael P. O'Shea. Thanks to Angelina's brother, Marco Petrucelli, Nico secured a position as a custodian in the office building. Marco had worked for the building manager for years, and this connection provided Nico not only with a job but also with critical skills for his new life in America. Both Angelina and Marco were learning English, and Marco mentioned, "For some reason, my sister is a bit hesitant to embrace English." He paused and then added, "I may not know your future plans, Nico, but let me tell you this: for you to thrive here, two things are essential." Nico listened attentively, eager to learn from Marco's wisdom.

"Become fluent in English and pursue an education." He was serious and sincere, Nico thought. Marco continued, "I myself am attending what they call night school. I am learning a lot there. In addition to this, I am also learning the language. You don't have to abandon your native language; just make an effort to learn the language of this country. Unless you want to fail," he added. This made sense to Nico. He knew he must not fail. "How can I enroll in school and learn the language?" he asked. Marco smiled broadly. His young protégé seemed well-motivated, and that was the first step on the journey to success. Nico worked about five hours a day. The lawyers at the firm took a liking to him, recognizing his sincerity, honesty, and strong work ethic. Despite the serious language barrier, Nico was motivated to succeed and seldom spoke to the lawyers. In the meantime, as promised, Marco decided for Nico to enroll in night school. What Nico discovered was that what his mentor referred to as night school was an informal group of immigrants being taught the basics in the home of a retired public school teacher named Agnes McGladrey. In her seventies, Agnes had a genuine desire to help immigrants navigate the challenges of assimilating into American society. Nico noticed that several other Italians were in his class, along with immigrants who spoke German, Spanish, and even Slovakian. Upon meeting Agnes McGladrey, Nico listened attentively as she spoke, with Marco translating for him. "Young man, I have made room for you in this class because Marco made a compelling case for your inclusion," she said, waiting for Marco to translate. "I really don't have much more room," she continued, "but he has convinced me that you are motivated and want to learn." Nico paid close attention to Marco's translation while his dark eyes remained fixed on the elderly woman. He nodded in agreement. "I hope that you will apply yourself," she said, pausing before asking what might have seemed like a premature question. "What do you think you would like to be here in America?" Without hesitation, the youngest son of one of Sicily's most notorious crime families replied, "Un Avvocato" (A lawyer).

As 1896 unfolded, Salvatore, along with his wife, child, and Nico Arcuri, embraced exciting changes in their new life as immigrants in a land full of possibilities. Salvatore devoted the early months of the year to building the foundation for his dream of leading his own "familia" in South Bethlehem. With charm and persuasion, he successfully enlisted John Capuano as a partner to create a "front" business. Salvatore knew John was too talented to be stuck on the railroad and skillfully highlighted the benefits of independence. "You truly deserve this opportunity," he encouraged, guiding John into this unexpected partnership. The next challenge for Salvatore was securing a prime spot in the bustling

Municipal Market. He set his sights on farmer Jacob Heckewelder, a man rooted in American tradition with a vast forty-acre farm in Lower Saucon Township. Although the details of how Salvatore convinced Heckewelder remain a bit of a mystery, by fall 1896, he had successfully claimed the market space and arranged for the farmer to supply goods for "Capuano's Stand." Salvatore proved that he was still a master of navigating challenges with confidence and strategy!

Soon after, the farmer was accepting an upfront payment of one hundred dollars and an enticing promise: every month from March to October, he would earn two percent of the stand's revenue. In no time, a new sign was proudly erected at stand number 68 in the bustling market, heralding the start of an exhilarating chapter for Salvatore, who was stepping into a genuine business opportunity for the first time. While Salvatore preferred to remain behind the scenes, John Capuano and the farmer took center stage, becoming the driving forces of what was soon to blossom into a flourishing enterprise. As John Capuano left the clangor of his railroad job behind, he felt a surge of renewed purpose and enthusiasm. The jubilant cheers and heartfelt congratulations from his fellow Italian community members acted like fuel for his spirit, uplifting him even further. Embracing this fresh identity as a budding entrepreneur, John immersed himself in the warm atmosphere of camaraderie and excitement that surrounded the stand. Meanwhile, Salvatore carefully attended to all the intricate details—inventory management, customer relations, and marketing strategies—ensuring everything ran smoothly. It wasn't long before the stand became a hive of activity, with patrons flocking to experience its offerings. The air was filled with the delightful aromas of fresh produce, while laughter and chatter thrived, creating a vibrant tapestry of energy and success at this market spot. Together, John and Salvatore transformed stand number 68 into the most sought-after destination, symbolizing the fulfillment of their hard work, vision, and dreams. Eventually, sensing that Salvatore had a Midas touch in the world of business, John Capuano gave in to just about every one of Salvatore's ideas, trusting him implicitly.

Agnes McGladrey sat at her kitchen table, reviewing the assignments submitted by her night school students. As usual, within three months, approximately half of the enrollees had abandoned their dream of learning and assimilating into American society. After five years of running this program, Agnes understood the reasons. For many immigrants, the transition was challenging, and in some cases, it felt impossible. The single biggest obstacle to learning was acquiring English-speaking skills. Years in the teaching profession had made Agnes acutely aware that learning English was difficult due to its complex pronunciation, inconsistent spelling patterns, a large vocabulary filled with irregular words, a variety of verb tenses, and confusing idioms and phrasal verbs. The presence of different dialects, which can vary significantly in pronunciation and word usage, further complicates the language. Essentially, many aspects of English do not follow clear rules, making it a daunting task for learners to master. If it proved difficult for native-born Americans, it could be nearly impossible for adult immigrants. However, some individuals displayed exceptional abilities. Agnes was currently reading a composition by her standout student, Nico Arcuri.

In a relatively short period of several months, the young man from Sicily had become her most accomplished student, particularly due to his reading comprehension skills. Agnes recognized that a percentage of students could grasp language concepts more easily than others, and Nico belonged to that group. As she read his essay about the American Civil War, she was struck by his quick understanding of the causes of the war and his almost flawless articulation of the conclusion in written English. Additionally, Nico demonstrated a remarkable aptitude for conversational language. Agnes felt tempted to congratulate herself for being such a wonderful teacher, but she acknowledged the probable truth: Nico Arcuri might genuinely be gifted.

As time passed, Michael O'Shea, the owner of the law firm Michael P. O'Shea and Associates, began to take notice of the young immigrant beyond his role as a custodian. Michael observed that in addition to being polite, dependable, and efficient, Nico seemed to possess an inner drive that impressed him greatly. Nico always carried a bag with him, which contained his lunch and one or two books. One day, intrigued by the janitor's reading habits, Michael approached Nico for the first time with a question.

O'Shea spoke slowly and deliberately as if addressing a three-year-old child. He assumed that this immigrant had little understanding of the English language, misinterpreting Nico's reticence as a lack of intellect.

"I was won-der-ing… what is the book that you are read-ing?" Nico looked up and replied, "It is 'The Kreutzer Sonata' by Leo Tolstoy." Michael O'Shea was stunned by the young man's command of the language as well as his choice of reading material. He had heard of the book, a novella, but was fascinated that this person would choose it and seemed to understand its content. Nico added, "Among other things, it discusses how marriage should be based on love and should never be arranged…" The next sentence out of O'Shea's mouth seemed to communicate with a peer. "I know this story and found it to be interesting. What drew you to this book, if I might ask?"

Nico marked his page, closed the book, and replied, "Where I come from, all marriages are arranged. Some are successful, but most, I believe, fail." His certainty shocked O'Shea. Nico continued, "As for where I obtained the book, I got it from Miss Agnes. She is my teacher." "That wouldn't be Agnes McGladrey, would it?" "Yes. My teacher," Nico said proudly. After they briefly discussed Nico's job and O'Shea acknowledged that he was doing good work, Michael O'Shea left Nico to finish his lunch. He then headed to the home of Agnes McGladrey.

Over cups of tea in her kitchen, O'Shea and Agnes McGladrey discussed her prize pupil. O'Shea himself had been a student of Agnes's during his grammar school days. Upon hearing how impressed O'Shea was with Nico, she admitted that she could only take so much credit. "Nico is about the most motivated student I have had the good fortune to encounter," said the veteran teacher. "In my years of mentoring immigrants in this program, I have perhaps met one or two who match him in desire, and none with his intellect." "Are you aware that he works at my office building?" asked Michael. "Doing what?" Agnes responded.

"I'm almost ashamed to say that he is working as a custodian." He paused, waiting for Miss McGladrey's response. "I'd say he is not working at a level commensurate with his intellect," she understated. "I could not agree more, madame. And I have an idea of how this may be remedied," he said. Once again, Nico Arcuri, the young man whose life had been turned upside down by events beyond his control, was about to receive an unexpected gift. For some time, O'Shea had pondered the strategy of expanding his law practice to include Immigration Law. He realized there was a growing need to address the rights and obligations of the increasing number of people entering the country, especially in a port town like Providence. Until now, no law firm has provided this service. A quick overview of the city revealed that approximately 80 to 90% of the immigrants arriving at the port were from Italy. In the past, O'Shea & Associates had been forced to turn away Italian-speaking immigrants. A light bulb went off in his head. "If only we had a bilingual employee—one who mastered both English and Italian and also had the intellect to be trained in law." Unbeknownst to the attorney, the answer to his question had been working in his building for many months.

With the blessing of Agnes McGladrey, Michael O'Shea was offering Nico Arcuri a new job and the opportunity of a lifetime. Nico felt somewhat intimidated as he sat in the private office of Michael O'Shea. The office was large, paneled with fine dark wood, and had two towering bookcases along one wall. A large window behind O'Shea's desk provided a view of the harbor beyond. Nico chose a chair facing the impressive desk.

"Nico, please relax. I have something very important to discuss with you today." As O'Shea lit a cigar, he offered one to his guest. Nico's mind raced, wondering if he had done something wrong. "No thank you," Nico replied, declining the cigar. "I have spoken with Miss McGladrey, and she has confirmed your character and your aptitude. I can also vouch for your sobriety and work ethic." Nico was unfamiliar with the term "work ethic." "Work ethic," O'Shea explained, "refers to one's values and the inner guide that influences how one approaches their job or work." Nico understood and appreciated the compliment. O'Shea recounted his conversation with the teacher and explained his idea to help immigrants, particularly those from Italy.

"There is a significant need for assistance because many come here from your country. I want to provide this support more effectively, which is why I need someone who can speak both English and Italian. Does that make sense to you?" "What do you see me doing to help?" Nico asked. "At first, I want you to translate documents, but I believe that with some guidance, you can become a lawyer." Nico had contemplated such a profession before, and while the idea of helping his fellow Italian immigrants was appealing, it felt like an impossible dream, especially for someone like him, even in America. O'Shea reassured him that with his support, achieving that dream was entirely possible. During the 1890s, most lawyers had neither attended college nor law school, as many states allowed class time to substitute for required apprenticeship hours. Most individuals became lawyers through independent study of classical legal texts, supplemented by apprenticeship and clerkships under the guidance of experienced attorneys. Under Michael O'Shea's mentorship, a bright young man like Nico Arcuri had a genuine opportunity to become a practicing attorney, focusing first on immigration law, and potentially more in the future. By 1897, Nico would begin his apprenticeship and clerkship at the law office of Michael P. O'Shea.

Chapter 23:
Eighteen Ninety-Seven

At the midpoint of 1897, the lives of brothers Salvatore and Nico had taken dramatic turns. Salvatore, now twenty-seven years old, had long since put behind him the self-inflicted troubles of Sicily. He rarely thought of the deaths of his parents, his sister, and presumably his younger brother. After arriving in America, he settled in South Bethlehem, Pennsylvania. Through cunning and ruthless determination, he had evaded death, assumed a new identity, and was now prepared to send for his wife and young son. Concetta, nearly twenty years old, had not seen her husband since his departure. She was unaware of the life he was preparing for her and their son, but any uncertainty she felt about moving to America was lessened by her trust in his judgment. She was also extremely happy that her mother and brother would be joining her. Salvatore's initial dream was to never work for anyone but himself and to dominate others, fully ready to straddle the line between law and disorder. In contrast, Nico's life was taking an entirely different path. He had settled in Providence, Rhode Island, and found several mentors. From Angelina Petrucelli to her brother and then to a kind teacher and a local attorney, the younger son of Il Leone greatly benefited from random connections with strangers. Nico shared several physical characteristics with his older brother: both were tall and slender, with dark, wavy hair and classic Sicilian features, such as square jawlines, prominent noses, thick dark brows, and olive complexions. Additionally, both were highly intelligent.

However, their similarities ended there. In terms of personality, the two were quite different. Salvatore was quick-tempered and often made impulsive decisions. One example was his decision to kill the farmer Neri, which led to a vendetta that splintered the Arcuri Crime Family and resulted in the deaths of his own family members. Even in South Bethlehem, he displayed these tendencies, unable or unwilling to see his arrival in America as an opportunity to change his ways. Nico, on the other hand, exhibited traits of what could be described as an echoist. Unlike his brother, he was skilled at understanding the feelings and needs of others. Perhaps his childhood illness, along with this trait, led both his father and brother to perceive him as "weak and soft." To the macho men of Sicily, this was a trait to be ashamed of. Regardless, Nico's qualities drew people to him, and they wanted to help him. This fundamental difference in their characters steered him toward the law and a selfless duty to others. He was capable of listening to others, measuring his thoughts and actions carefully. His respectful and deliberate manner suggested that he would remain on the side of the law. The journey from the port of Naples to Ellis Island took place in late October 1897. Concetta Maria Teggiano was accompanied by her two-year-old son Amato, her fifty-one-year-old mother Antoinette Fisco, and her soon-to-be eighteen-year-old brother Anthony. They were well-prepared for the trip, thanks to the experiences of Carlo Zollo, Giovanni Capuano, and Salvatore. The ship, named "The Antenor," was relatively new. The Teggiano family was fortunate, as Salvatore ensured that their passage was more comfortable than his had been. He paid for first-class accommodations, so the four immigrants found themselves in rooms on the upper deck that were less confining and offered a degree of privacy. While not luxurious, Salvatore made certain that his family would be comfortable during the two-week journey. Along the way, Concetta reviewed the "process" they could expect upon arriving at Ellis Island. Everyone memorized the procedure, preparing themselves as best as possible for what awaited them. Salvatore felt genuine excitement to see his beautiful wife and the son he barely knew.

On October 23rd, as they arrived at the lively port of New York, Salvatore and John Capuano eagerly awaited the arrival of Concetta and the others. The processing went smoothly, and soon they were excitedly aboard a train, embarking on a one-hundred-mile journey west toward their new home. Salvatore held his son close for the first time, overwhelmed with emotion. Amato gazed up at his father, feeling a mix of curiosity and uncertainty about this new connection. Concetta enthusiastically repeated, "Amato, Questo è tuo padre!"—"Amato, this is your father!" As the family opened the thoughtful gifts from Salvatore, John took the opportunity to share the inspiring story of his journey in America. He proudly described his successful business partnership with Salvatore, exuding optimism about their accomplishments. "Concetta, you're going to be so proud of all that we've achieved in such a short time! Our business is thriving, and we have a wonderful home ready for you!" he exclaimed with genuine enthusiasm. "And, Anthony, we've thought of you too!" John shared exciting news about an apprenticeship he had arranged for Anthony with a barber on Fourth Street. "Signior Casamassa owes me a favor and would be delighted to train you!" Capuano explained, radiating encouragement. Anthony listened with a mix of appreciation and concern. "Why does he think I want to be a barber?" he pondered, but he managed to smile and replied sincerely, "Grazie." This was the start of their new adventure in a land filled with possibilities!

Settling into their new house on Vine Street, Concetta and her mother were overwhelmed by the unfamiliar sights, sounds, and customs of South Bethlehem. The language barrier was a significant obstacle for both. However, they were impressed by how much John and Salvatore had mastered basic English, and John, in particular, worked with them to help them learn the new language. "Fortunately, there are many Italians here and quite a few from Foiano," John assured them. Antoinette's questions mostly revolved around her faith and practical matters, such as where to find food. "Is there a church?" she asked. "Of course," John replied. "There is a Catholic church just four blocks from here." He was referring to Holy Infancy Parish, the first Roman Catholic church in town. "It is beautiful. I have been there." John purposely left out the detail that this Irish church did not exactly welcome other immigrants, including Italians. In fact, the Italians were in the process of petitioning the archdiocese for an Italian-speaking priest to be sent to South Bethlehem. They even dreamed of building their own church. Salvatore listened but was indifferent to John's church aspirations. He shrugged when Concetta glanced at him. "Concetta, come with me. I have something to show you," he said. Salvatore took his wife's hand as they navigated the busy streets, leading them approximately five blocks to the impressive building where Salvatore and John had established their business. "Here it is—the market house," he proclaimed proudly. Once inside, Concetta was overwhelmed by a mix of odors that were difficult to identify. She recognized the smell of chickens, both fresh and unpleasant, as well as fish, and a faint odor that might have been urine. Additionally, she detected the scent of cigar smoke. The large space was filled with endless rows of wooden stalls. Most were staffed, while a few stood vacant. Soon, Salvatore pointed out a stall with a sign above it that read "J. Capuano—Fine Fruits, Vegetables." Manning the stand was an elderly woman.

"Behold, my dearest, our grand enterprise," Salvatore declared, his voice a mixture of pride and ambition. Concetta stood there, somewhat bewildered, caught between admiration and uncertainty as her husband continued. "In just six short months, we have crafted a truly remarkable business. Can you believe it? Nearly $2,000 in profit!" he exclaimed, his eyes gleaming with excitement. To Concetta, an Italian immigrant still trying to grasp the full weight of American currency, those numbers were abstract, a faint echo of significance. Yet, Salvatore was right to bask in his achievement; in 1897, $2,000 held the staggering value of nearly fifty thousand dollars in today's economy! However, what Salvatore chose to withhold from his unsuspecting bride was the dark truth lurking beneath the surface of their success. More than half of that wealth trickling through their business was tainted, derived from the illicit operations belonging to Salvatore's true enterprise. With a cunning that belied his charming exterior, he preyed upon the unsuspecting townsfolk, calculating that the local law enforcement, many of whom were Irish, would turn a blind eye to the "petty crimes" plaguing the Italian community. Stripped of protection and caught in a spiral of sudden lawlessness, the Italians felt vulnerable and confused. The genius of Salvatore's scheme lay in his ability to gather a band of thugs from his own community, mostly young, unemployed, and uneducated men desperate for cash. Under the cloak of respectability, he orchestrated a gang that extorted money from terrified merchants, demanding "protection from misfortune." Those who dared to defy him were met with swift and brutal retribution – broken windows, threats, and even physical violence. Meanwhile, a sprinkle of bribes for the local officers ensured that any reports of these crimes quietly vanished, leaving the Italian business community shrouded in mystery and fear. To them, Salvatore appeared as a pillar of society, a benevolent businessman hiding the malicious intent behind his smile. In no time, he had amassed a small army, and intriguingly, his influence began to reach beyond the Italian enclave, ensnaring disenchanted Irish youths as well. The more money flowed into Salvatore's coffers, the more power he wielded, and he envisioned a future where he could even buy the silence of judges. By 1898, Salvatore Teggiano's fruit stand became a nexus for cash that came from varied and sordid enterprises, including a dubious street lottery and the exploitation of women in prostitution. His uncanny instincts about not just America but this industrial town's pulse proved correct. Working men, weary from their struggles, seemed all too eager to dissipate their hard-earned wages upon receiving them, almost as if it were a race against time to part with their pay before returning home. Salvatore often chuckled to himself, darkly amused, observing that as these men toiled for meager sums, they encountered countless opportunities to squander their earnings before even setting foot back in their homes. He felt it was his duty, almost a calling, to liberate them from their hard-earned money. Some succumbed to gambling temptations, others to the allure of loose women, while many surrendered their paychecks to the incessant tide of taverns sprouting up on every corner of South Bethlehem. Though Salvatore tightly gripped the reins of gambling and prostitution, the tantalizing alcohol business loomed just out of reach. He pondered the potential profits, deliberating over this lucrative venture, yet felt no urgency to dive in just yet. "Tomorrow's another day…" he mused, the wheels of ambition and opportunism turning in his mind. One thing was undeniable in this land of opportunity: anything was indeed possible.

Chapter 24:
Two Brothers, Two Very Different Paths

At the turn of the century, the old world that Salvatore and his brother had left behind had changed very little since they arrived in America. In the six years since Salvatore and Nico had found themselves fleeing for their lives, their lives had changed dramatically, and depending on one's perspective, much for the better. In the impoverished region of Campania/Benevento, however, the citizens of Foiano di Val Fortore saw no appreciable difference in their circumstances. "Born poor, die poor" was their saying, as it had been for countless generations. In Sicily, poverty and violence reigned supreme. The once-powerful Arcuri crime family had been scattered. None of the surviving members were willing to fight for their criminal fortunes. Following the assassination of Armando Loggia, with all the top five members of the clan's hierarchy out of the way, Don Pedrotti declared that the vendetta was over. The remaining members were allowed to live as peaceful, powerless peasants.

By contrast, in 1900, South Bethlehem continued to thrive. Trains ran around and through the area day and night. The ironworks had transitioned into a steel company, and its furnaces belched out noise and soot all day long. Third Street was alive with activity; every imaginable type of business seemed to be located there. The immigrant population was growing not only in numbers but also in diversity. This place had become a true "melting pot." Working and living side by side were the Irish, Italians, Poles, Greeks, Hungarians, Slavs, and Slovenians. Practically all were Catholic, and nearly all were at least religiously observant. In no time, churches rivaled taverns as prominent landmarks in the South Bethlehem landscape. In 1901, after much prayer to Saint John the Hermit, the growing Foianese population worked diligently to obtain permission from the Philadelphia archdiocese to build an Italian church. Even before the church had a physical structure, it had a name: Our Lady of Pompeii of the Most Holy Rosary, or Madonna di Pompei Santissima Rosario. The church would be built on Fourth Street, not far from where many Foianese had settled. A plot of land had been donated and was consecrated, and despite having limited resources, the community constructed their church using stones and other materials salvaged from a recently demolished public school. The church rose in the 800 block of East Fourth Street in 1902. The announcement of the new church was met with great joy, especially by Concetta's mother.

By 1902, Concetta was pregnant with what would be her third child. She and Salvatore had welcomed a second child within the first year of Concetta's arrival, a daughter they named Theresa Maria. The christening of the third baby was one of the very first ceremonies held at the new parish. The growth of the Italian population, particularly the Foianese, demonstrated their adaptive nature in America. They quickly learned that to achieve real progress, immigrants needed to assimilate into American culture and acquire political power. They took lessons from the Irish, who, unburdened by a language barrier, had made significant inroads into political life. Following the Irish example, the Italians began by becoming ward leaders. Nearly every Italian registered to vote, with the vast majority choosing the Worker's Party and becoming proud Democrats. For most Foianese, this path to power and respectability unfolded naturally. They intended to play by the rules in their new homeland.

In contrast, Salvatore Teggiano accepted none of these limitations. Politicians were merely obstacles in his pursuit of American success. He cynically assessed the leaders, their police, and even the judges, deducing, as his father had taught him, that "Every man has his price." By 1905, Salvatore's influence over the borough of South Bethlehem had become nearly a stranglehold. 1905 was also the year Salvatore and Concetta welcomed their fourth and final child, a son they named Frank Dominick Teggiano.

The revenue flowing into Salvatore's hands from the *J. Capuano-Fine Fruits and Vegetables* enterprise was quite impressive. Salvatore ensured that approximately twenty-five percent of his ill-gotten gains were recorded as "sales" on the company ledgers, while the rest was pocketed for miscellaneous expenses. By this time, he and his family had moved out of the Vine Street home they shared with John and into a new house on Hillside Avenue, located on the eastern end of the borough near the Lehigh University campus. This was a "single home," which signified a level of status unusual for someone so recently arrived. The location pleased Antoinette, primarily because it placed them much closer to the church. In addition to this home purchase, Salvatore invested in several legitimate ventures that benefited the Italian community. A loan office had opened at the corner of Third Street and Elm, followed by a bank located at Fourth and Spruce—both enterprises were built by and meant for Italians.

In South Bethlehem, Salvatore was managing to hide in plain sight, and this pleased him. Unlike his father, he ruled less through intimidation and more by "influencing" those around him. Although he could not resist a life of crime in his adopted home, it appeared that he was learning to control his more destructive impulses, for the most part. By this time, at thirty-five years old, he was married with four young children. Despite living on the wrong side of the law, he had to be considered successful. Il Leone's first son's version of the family business was less brutal but even more effective. Salvatore had grudgingly accepted the model of Don Pedrotti, which positioned the head of the family in a reputable station, creating an aura of respectability. This allowed Salvatore to perform without the need to place himself in harm's way. The soldiers that he commanded took the outward risks. Sworn to secrecy regarding who they were working for, Salvatore operated confidently. A significant portion of the money his enterprises produced was reinvested by purchasing influence. This protection would safeguard his nefarious initiatives.

Although Salvatore was extremely careful and consistent in guarding against the vices that had once provided his livelihood—foregoing gambling, drinking, and drug use—he had begun to develop a habit that was becoming potentially problematic. By this time, Salvatore had started keeping mistresses.

Success for Francesco Arcuri's second son, Nico, was measured quite differently. By 1906, Nico was a twenty-eight-year-old intern, training and assisting in the law office of Michael O'Shea. O'Shea initially brought Nico along slowly, but he soon recognized that his protégé was a quick learner. Nico absorbed knowledge rapidly and was quickly elevated from bi-lingual assistant to *special assistant to Michael O'Shea*. Nico's language skills were so impressive that O'Shea had no hesitation in trusting him to interact with clients, regardless of the language they spoke. Soon, Nico was handling various administrative tasks and was entrusted with legal research, document preparation, case preparation, and the aspect he loved most—trial support. It was during this trial support role, seated next to his mentor in the courtroom, that Nico realized becoming a trial lawyer was his true aspiration. He pictured himself sparring with a worthy adversary, putting into practice what he had been learning. But was he ready?

The two men were having lunch at the Barrister's Club, located not far from their office. Nico was captivated by the surroundings: the cherry paneling, leather-backed chairs, fine china, and the smell of cigars. Michael O'Shea's invitation for lunch was a significant milestone in Nico's professional career. The club was exclusive to lawyers, and seeing the inside was something Nico had only imagined prior to receiving his invitation. "What are your thoughts?" Michael O'Shea asked. Nico paused and then whispered, "I'm very impressed, but I feel somewhat unworthy." "You would never have been invited if you were unworthy,

Nico." Nico took a sip of his first glass of Scotch whisky, as recommended by his mentor. He disliked it and apologized to Michael, saying, "I—I don't care much for it." Michael O'Shea smiled and said, "That's one of the things I appreciate about you, Nico. You are refreshingly honest to a fault. In fact, I'm not sure if that trait will serve you well as you pursue a career in law." The two men laughed.

During their lunch meeting, Michael leaned in slightly, his voice low as he disclosed the reason for their gathering. "I wanted to take another moment to express my gratitude for your invaluable help in preparing for the Grady Trial."

The trial in question involved an Irish immigrant, Martin Grady, who found himself facing a murder charge following a chaotic and drunken altercation in a smoky tavern, where tempers flared and ultimately led to the tragic death of another man. "Your extensive research and crucial contributions played a significant role in persuading the jury to see that Mr. Grady was acting in self-defense during a fight instigated by the deceased," Michael stated, his eyes reflecting the weight of the case. Nico felt a wave of pride wash over him as he recognized that his instincts had notably impacted the case's outcome.

His relentless pursuit of truth led him to uncover the testimony of a previously uncooperative witness, whose revelations prompted the jury to reconsider the murder accusation and focus instead on the self-defense argument. Because of this pivotal testimony, Martin Grady emerged from the courtroom not guilty of the more severe murder charge. While Michael O'Shea stood before the jury, delivering compelling arguments and basking in the accolades that followed, he understood the vital role that Nico had played behind the scenes. "To me, you are nothing less than a lawyer," Michael insisted with sincerity. "Of course, there are still challenges ahead, including the necessity of presenting a case independently..." The phrase "By yourself" struck Nico like a cold gust of wind. Although he had been a steadfast aide to the seasoned lawyer, garnering a solid understanding of legal concepts and courtroom procedures, the thought of soloing a case was daunting and stirred a sense of dread within him. Noticing the flicker of apprehension in Nico's eyes, Michael quickly reassured him. "Don't let it trouble you. If I didn't have unwavering confidence in your abilities, I wouldn't have come this far alongside you. You're ready, my friend." The faith that Michael O'Shea placed in him ignited a spark of invincibility in Nico Arcuri, brightening his resolve.

After the workday concluded, Nico returned to the warm and welcoming home he shared with the Petrucelli family. Angelina greeted him with infectious pride and joy as she absorbed the news of his achievements. She embraced him tightly, planting a soft kiss on his cheek. "I have watched you transform and grow so much over these past ten years!" she exclaimed, her voice ringing with affection. The conversation flowed easily between them in English, a language that had become second nature to Nico. As he gazed at Angelina, a flood of realization washed over him; an entire decade had slipped by since his arrival in the United States. Looking closely at her face, he noticed the subtle lines that told stories of joy and hardship—details he had somehow overlooked before. The once-lustrous black hair of the fifty-year-old women now bore streaks of gray, each strand a testament to the passage of time. It struck him profoundly that those around him were also evolving, aging in ways he had yet to fully acknowledge. At that moment, he recognized with clarity that he, too, had undergone significant changes far beyond his expectations. At just twenty-eight years old, Nico Arcuri had achieved a remarkable level of success that many immigrants longed for, but only a fortunate few would ever realize.

On June 17th, 1921, Nico Arcuri, a surviving son and brother of two notorious criminal masterminds took his oath to become a lawyer.

The path that Nico had chosen was as different from that of his older brother as night is to day. As explained to him by his mentor Michael O'Shea, taking the so-called Attorney's Oath was short, sweet and of course, necessary, so in Courtroom number Three within the Providence County Courthouse, Nico recited the pledge, hand on bible.

"I, Nico Arcuri, do solemnly and sincerely promise and swear that I will truly and faithfully, and to the best of my skill and knowledge, execute the powers and trusts reposed in me as Attorney at Law, so help me God."

The partners and staff at the Michael P. O'Shea law firm were on hand to witness the achievement. Also present was a member of Nico's surrogate family, Angelina Petrucelli.

Michael spoke.

"I am certain that all present join me in congratulating Nico on this remarkable achievement." He turned toward the honoree, "Nico, it is customary for a person in this circumstance to say a few words".

Nico cleared his throat. As he scanned the room, he felt a flood of emotions.

"I need to thank Judge Morgan, and all the people at our firm, and of course, my very special thanks to Mr. O'Shea, whose unwavering support has sustained me along this journey." Nico heard light sobbing. It was Angelina.

He asked for the woman to step forward and to join him. Placing his arm around the now frail woman, he spoke again.

"I should begin by saying, none of this would have been possible were it not for Angelina. From our very first meeting, she accepted me and believed in me. So, it is with great humility and gratitude that I express my deepest thanks to her."

He continued. "You know, I am also in need to keep in my mind the contributions of those no longer with me. Miss Agnes McGladrey, who nurtured my curiosity and who taught me so many things. To Marco who counseled me, and even to that processor at the port of entry who was kind to me and helped me enter the country." Angelina smiled at that memory.

"And I would be remiss not to remember my parents, my sister and my brother" ... he choked back tears. No one had ever heard Nico speak about his family.

"They are all here today, in spirit at least..."

In the next several months, Michael O'Shea worked diligently to assist Nico in setting up his own office. Unexpectedly, the newly minted lawyer declined an offer to officially join the O'Shea law firm. Having gotten to know Nico over the years, he was not totally surprised by this decision. He realized that Nico had a strong desire to become independent, after so many years of dependency, first to the Petrucellis, then to Miss Agnes McGladrey, and especially to O'Shea. Nico was proud, and although he greatly appreciated the many kindnesses that he had received, he was most anxious to strike out on his own. Perhaps this was one commonality that he shared with his father and his older brother. Like the others, Nico felt a strong instinct to become independent of others; unlike them, he found himself firmly on the side of law and order.

Sunday, December 9th, 1921, was moving day for Nico Arcuri, Attorney at Law. With the help of a small army of acquaintances and friends, office furniture and law books were brought into his new office. Located on the first floor of a three-story brownstone building that Nico had purchased a year earlier, the space was taking shape. "331 Weybosset Street," he was heard saying into the telephone as he finalized a delivery for a desk he had purchased. This desk represented his single largest investment for the office, totaling $350.00. At that time, it seemed like an extravagant sum to spend so early in his career, but Nico remembered how impressive his mentor appeared seated behind his oak desk. He believed that having a distinguished office was crucial for building a successful clientele.

As Angelina entered the room, she was greeted by the smell of fresh paint. Being a spinster, Nico was as close as she could come to experiencing the joy of motherhood. She felt a swell of maternal pride as she observed his growth, both as a man and a successful citizen. Angelina had taken a chance on the lonely, lost boy and nurtured him until he could find stability. She sensed that her fellow Sicilian had the potential for success, and her instincts had proven to be accurate. Nico greeted Angelina in Italian, but soon they transitioned to the language of their new homeland. "Angelina, come stai, mia cara?" ("Angelina, how are you, my dear?") "Sono vecchio, ma felice!" ("I am old, but happy!") Grabbing her hands, Nico kissed her on each cheek. "What do you think of my office?" he asked. "Bello, bello," she replied, looking around at the pile of law books scattered across the floor. "And what will become of these books?" "I'll soon sort and organize them and place them on the shelves. They are perhaps my most important tools," he said. Angelina then handed Nico a small box wrapped in tissue paper. "A gift for my new lawyer," she said as she presented it to him. "This wasn't necessary, Zia Angelina," Nico replied, though he accepted her thoughtful tribute. He had long referred to the kindly woman as "Zia," meaning Aunt, out of affection. As he unwrapped the package, Nico found himself holding a BCHR Conklin Crescent Model 20P fountain pen. He recognized it immediately as a favored choice among the legal community he knew. He also realized that the pen, featuring a gold nib and premium features, cost an extravagant $21.00—far too much for Zia Angelina to spend on her modest earnings. "Nonsense," she reassured him, insisting that such an investment was well within her ability. "I want you to have something nice to commemorate this achievement." Nico examined the pen closely. Inscribed on it were the words, "For Nico, with deepest love and pride, Zia Angelina."

To Nico Arcuri, Angelina Petrucelli was more than just a surrogate family member; she was, for all intents and purposes, his mother, and she was just one of several people he had encountered in America to whom he felt gratitude and for whom he wanted to reward by succeeding in his chosen field.

His first opportunity to prove himself presented itself very soon.

In the vibrant streets of Providence, Rhode Island, during the early twentieth century, Italian immigrants navigated a myriad of challenges, from economic struggles to societal biases. Yet, in the heart of this setting emerged a remarkable Sicilian immigrant named Nico Arcuri, whose journey would not only shape his career but also uplift his entire community. Nico arrived in America towards the tail end of the nineteenth century, a time when the influx of Italian immigrants was at an all-time high. Many of his fellow countrymen were fueled by dreams of a brighter future, and Nico was no exception. However, his dreams were paired with a sense of urgency; he was also escaping peril back home. While many immigrants found work in labor-intensive jobs, Nico was determined to chart a different course. With a deep-rooted passion for justice and a sharp mind, he set his sights on becoming a lawyer—an ambitious goal considering the rampant discrimination Italians faced back then. Despite the societal hurdles, Nico's commitment to his education never wavered. He juggled a demanding day job while devoting his evenings to his studies. Gratefully, he received encouragement from the Petrucelli family and other community members, which played a crucial role in his remarkable journey. Nico's hard work paid off when he triumphantly passed the bar exam, a groundbreaking milestone for someone with his background. Yet, obtaining his license was just a steppingstone; winning the trust of clients in a field dominated by Anglo-Saxon professionals was an entirely different challenge.

Nico's first chance to shine as an independent attorney came when he represented Mrs. Antoinette Sontapietro, an Italian immigrant wrongfully accused of murdering Joseph Marino, a case that quickly drew widespread attention. Facing the possibility of the death penalty, Mrs. Sontapietro's situation was dire. Nico believed in her innocence and understood the barriers of language and culture that had complicated her initial trial. Perhaps his faith in her mirrored the unwavering support he had received from his Aunt Angelina. Throughout his journey, he learned that optimism and faith were powerful allies.

Through diligent research and a compassionate presentation of the cultural context, Nico proved that Mrs. Sontapietro had acted in self-defense. He uncovered pivotal evidence that had been misrepresented during her original trial due to poor translation. His relentless pursuit of justice reduced Mrs. Sontapietro's sentence from death to seven and a half years, highlighting the flaws of the earlier proceedings. This case was reminiscent of the Grady trial, yet this time, it was Nico who stood as the persuasive voice for justice.

Nico Arcuri's brilliant success in this case resonated profoundly within the Italian American community. He illustrated the necessity of competent legal representation while shedding light on the systemic challenges immigrants faced within the justice system. His victory sparkled as a beacon of hope, inspiring fellow Italian immigrants to stand up for their rights and motivating a new generation to consider careers in law. In a time filled with adversity, Nico exemplified the resilience and potential of immigrants striving to forge their own paths in America. The outcome of the Sontapietro trial captured the attention of the Providence legal community, who began to recognize the extraordinary talent of this young lawyer. Nico's journey is a heartwarming testament to the power of determination, community support, and unwavering faith in the possibility of change.

Nico Arcuri stepped into a world that seemed relentlessly hostile to a foreigner. The city's elite, steeped in their self-importance, dismissed him coldly; doors closed with a resounding finality as he approached. Yet, undeterred by the indifference that surrounded him, Nico carved out a modest office in the heart of the city, fueled by an unwavering resolve to triumph as an independent attorney. His initial clientele consisted of fellow immigrants—men unjustly accused of crimes they did not commit, and women yearning for justice in a society that had largely turned its back on them. Word of Nico's tenacity spread like wildfire, and as his reputation took flight, he became a beacon of hope for the oppressed. He radiated an infectious passion for defending the underdog, wielding a sharp legal intellect that echoed throughout the courtrooms. When Prohibition swept across the nation like a dark shadow, he found himself standing beside small-time bootleggers and beleaguered bar owners, swept away in the federal government's iron grip. With a fearless spirit and a sharp tongue, he delivered arguments that rang out with clarity and conviction, earning him the moniker—"The People's Lawyer"—in the press.

As the 1930s dawned, Nico's star ascended to dazzling heights; he had transformed into one of the most sought-after attorneys in Providence, his clientele now comprised of influential businessmen and politicians. Yet, despite his success, his heart stayed tethered to his roots. He often took on pro bono cases for immigrants facing the grim specter of deportation or wrongful imprisonment. To Nico, the law was a protective shield, a means to safeguard the vulnerable, and he wielded it with unparalleled finesse, like a maestro conducting a symphony of justice. Nico Arcuri's legacy wasn't merely built on his accolades but on an unwavering foundation of integrity. He stood steadfast against the allure of corruption, never allowing the trials of his youth to fade from memory. He fought tirelessly for those rendered voiceless in a city often blind to their plight. His name became synonymous with justice, resonating in the streets of Providence like a battle cry for the disenfranchised. Through it all, he kept Zia Angelina's fountain pen close, a cherished emblem of his remarkable journey—a journey that began with an arduous crossing on a ship bound for Ellis Island but found its pivotal chapter in Providence. It was the odyssey of a young boy who grew into a man, an immigrant who embraced his identity as an American, and a dreamer who blossomed into an enduring legend.

These two brothers, who had become separated years earlier, evolved in completely differing directions. While Salvatore was selfish and had a tendency toward criminal behavior, Nico was generous and principled. Salvatore was manipulative, almost enjoying the way he corrupted everything and everyone around him. In contrast, Nico was unpretentious and sincere, showing genuine care for others. These contrasts would define the remainder of their lives, creating a widening chasm that was impossible to bridge.

Chapter 25:
Nineteen-Twenty-Nine

By the year 1929, the two brothers had each endured the heavy toll of *destiny and fate*, their lives altered by a series of choices—most notably, those made by Salvatore. His impulsive decision set into motion a chain of events that neither brother could have possibly anticipated, leading them on divergent paths that would shape their futures in profound and unpredictable ways. One might argue that what ultimately became Salvatore's destiny morphed into Nico's fate, a consequence of their intertwined lives. Despite the turbulence resulting from his brother's actions, the younger Arcuri son, Nico, succeeded in upholding his name and true identity. Rising from humble beginnings,

Nico Arcuri faced numerous disappointments and hardships, yet he emerged as a prominent figure in his field. In the year 1894, the notion of becoming a lawyer had been merely a distant dream for him, but by 1929, he had cemented his status as a respected member of the legal community in Providence, Rhode Island, known for his unwavering dedication and sharp intellect.

As Salvatore sat in the elegantly adorned hall of Società di Mutuo Soccorso, the air filled with music and laughter, he found himself lost in thought, pondering the course of his own life—a journey that had become fraught with anguish and regret. He had intentionally chosen to follow a path laid out by their father, one rich in ambition yet perilous. Unfortunately, in pursuing that ambition, he had unwittingly orchestrated the death and devastation of their father and the disintegration of his once-flourishing organization. The toll on his personal relationships was staggering, costing the lives of friends and family alike. Although he managed to evade direct consequences by fleeing and remaining concealed, the price of survival had been the loss of his honor and integrity. As he gazed across the crowded room, he spotted the beautiful Concetta Maria, now transformed into a graceful fifty-year-old grandmother, sharing joyful moments on the dance floor with others. In that instant, it dawned on him that, among the many hollow accomplishments he had amassed, he had also deceived the very woman who had given him children. Every aspect of his identity—his name, his history—had been meticulously crafted lies designed to mask the truth. Furthermore, Salvatore came to realize that the empire he had successfully built in America was largely constructed upon the tenacity and humility he had long abandoned. His disdain for the so-called "piccoli uomini," or little men, had blinded him to their essential contributions. Yet, if these realizations stirred any genuine remorse within him, Salvatore remained adept at concealing such feelings. In his pursuit of power, he had knowingly corrupted his dear friend Gio Capuano, as well as his own son Amato. Both men, once innocent and kind-hearted, had been irrevocably changed by the vast corruption Salvatore had unleashed, their lives forever altered by the weight of his choices.

In his personal habits, Salvatore Teggiano was ensnared by greed, selfishness, and infidelity, particularly towards his devoted wife, Concetta. Long ago, he had surrendered to his desires, indulging in the embrace of various mistresses. As he gazed at the innocent woman whose love wrapped around him like a warm blanket, a mere flicker of regret stirred within him for the betrayal he so callously orchestrated. The lively party wound down as the clock struck eleven. Behind the facade of charm and confidence, Salvatore prepared to weave yet another thread of deception around Concetta. "John, see Concetta home for me," he instructed with a nonchalant wave, gesturing to his longtime friend, John Capuano. "I have some pressing business to attend to." "Of course," John replied, his loyalty unwavering. In the depths of his heart, John understood that Salvatore's "business" meant slipping away for a secret rendezvous with a woman who had captured his attention. The bond of secrecy between them was a fragile but reliable thread; Salvatore trusted John implicitly, a sentiment that was not reciprocated in full. John had known Salvatore for thirty-five years, and in that time, the two had forged a connection that few could rival. Yet, Salvatore maintained a veil of mystery around much of his past. One night, after settling into the warm, inviting atmosphere of a smoky bar, the two friends, buoyed by the spirit of camaraderie and drink, had plumbed deeper depths of their friendship. Under the influence of Grappa—the potent elixir distilled from the remnants of winemaking—Salvatore had, perhaps unwittingly, let slip fragments of his earlier life in Sicily. In that haze of intoxication, he revealed two unsettling truths to John: he had fabricated a story about his origins, and his true name was not Teggiano, but "Arcuri". Realizing he had unveiled too much, Salvatore swiftly shifted the conversation, leaving the truth hanging in the air like smoke. Yet months later, he issued a strange and chilling directive to John. "If I die... when I die, you must inscribe my tombstone with my real name. This secret must remain until that time; do you understand?" In truth, John felt a chilling uncertainty settle over him, but as always, he nodded and promised to comply, masking his confusion with a veneer of acceptance. Behind the bravado of Salvatore Teggiano lay an inner shame; he grappled with the weight of renouncing his identity, realizing that he had but one final chance to rectify his past transgressions. The walk from the bustling club on Mechanic Street to his residence on Second Street was a mere three blocks east, but to Salvatore, it felt like traversing a vast chasm filled with secrets. He waited patiently until Concetta departed with John, her naivete a comforting shroud. Salvatore's trust in John was steadfast; his trust in himself, however, was fraught with peril. Weeks prior, Salvatore had crossed paths with a captivating young woman named Bianca Morganello. At twenty-four, she was a stunning enchantress, her beauty marred only by a reputation that danced on the edges of propriety. This reckless charm was precisely what thrilled Salvatore; he craved the allure of youth, and Bianca ignited that craving within him. His secret trysts with her often unfolded in dimly lit hotel rooms across the north side of the city—places concealed from prying eyes. This evening, their illicit encounter would take place at her designated Second Street address, her promise echoing in his mind, steeped in temptation.

The police received the call at two o'clock in the morning. The crime scene was bloody and indicated anger, passion, possibly revenge as motives. The two bodies were in the bedroom. The lifeless and bloody body of Bianca Morganello was splayed across the bed. She had been stabbed numerous times.

On the floor, was the body of a nearly sixty-year-old man. His death was the result of numerous gunshots, including two to his head. He was later identified as Salvatore Teggiano.

The author of the final chapter of the life of the son of Il Leone was a nondescript twenty-five-year-old Sicilian immigrant from a town called Ragusa named Roberto Morano. As the police took him into custody, he revealed that Bianca was his wife.

For his part, John Capuano would go on to satisfy the promise that he made to his friend. As such, a modest tombstone was purchased, and upon it was inscribed the true family name of Salvatore. The monument would be placed in the hillside cemetery known as Saint Michael's in South Bethlehem, Pennsylvania.

This final action ended the destiny of Salvatore Francesco Arcuri.

Note

This is a work of fiction. The characters in this story are entirely fictional and are not intended to represent any actual individuals, living or deceased. While the locations mentioned are real, the author does not intend to connect this fictional story to any real places. "Two Brothers" aims to highlight the possible differences between siblings. Although genetics can help explain some resemblances between siblings, environmental factors primarily account for the rest. Children raised by the same parents may experience vastly different environments, both in terms of their perceptions and their actual circumstances.

Author's Note

As I contemplated ideas for my first novel, I found myself repeatedly reflecting on a piece of advice from a well-known and successful author who was once asked, "How does one know what to write about?" The author responded, "Always write about what you know, or at least what you are passionate or curious about." Guided by this wisdom, I decided to write "Two Brothers."

I have a strong interest in history and am passionate about my family lineage, having traced my genealogy in Italy back to the eighteenth century. As an only child, I have always been curious about something I could never experience: what it would be like to have a sibling. This curiosity formed the foundation of the novel you are about to read. The connective tissue that unites the elements of this story, which spans approximately sixty years in the characters' lives, is the distinction between fate and destiny.

While often used interchangeably, "fate" generally refers to a predetermined course of events beyond human control, suggesting a sense of helplessness. In contrast, "destiny" implies a more personal and potentially attainable future path, with the understanding that individuals can influence their outcomes through choices and actions. Essentially, "fate" is what happens to you, while "destiny" is what you actively create.

In "Two Brothers," we explore the paths taken by the main characters and come to realize that sometimes, one person's destiny may be shaped by another's fate.

I hope you enjoy this work of fiction.

Special thanks to Robert E. Corsi and Robert B. Ruyak.

About the Author

Mark C. Iampietro began writing as a hobby after his retirement from a forty-year career as a civil servant. Since 2016, he has authored numerous columns and essays, and he has published nine books that span various topics, including local history, children's literature, and even a cookbook. "Two Brothers" marks his debut in the realm of fiction.

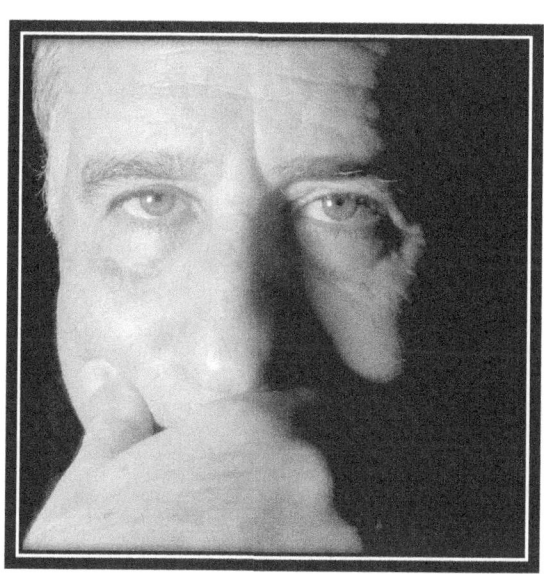

Made in the USA
Middletown, DE
19 March 2025